AQUARIUS
(January 20 to February 19)

The most humanitarian and peace-loving of signs, yet Aquarians have a knack for ending up in unpredictable, disruptive and unusual situations. They love mysteries and are well-known for their ability to see into the future. Aquarians are scientific, fascinated by new inventions and discoveries and will always try anything once.

Amber's project on telekinesis gets out of hand when she and a group of friends discover they have the power to move things – without touching them. Then Amber has disturbing dreams – and these dreams seem to come true. Does she alone have the power to make things happen for the good...as well as for revenge?

ZODIAC

*Whatever your sun sign, you'll want to read
Zodiac, the series written in the stars.*

SERIES CREATED BY JAHNNA N. MALCOLM

ZODIAC

AQUARIUS

SECOND SIGHT

JAHNNA N. MALCOLM

Lions

An Imprint of HarperCollinsPublishers

First published in Lions in 1995

Lions is an imprint of CollinsChildren'sBooks,
a Division of HarperCollins*Publishers* Ltd,
77-85 Fulham Palace Road, Hammersmith, London W6 8JB

1 3 5 7 9 8 6 4 2

Copyright © Jahnna N. Malcolm 1995

The author asserts the moral right to be
identified as the author of the work

ISBN: 0 00 675048 6

Printed and bound in Great Britain by
HarperCollins Manufacturing Ltd, Glasgow.

For Allie, Natalie, Willa,
and Chip the Love Dog.

CHAPTER ONE

AQUARIUS (January 20 – February 19)
Moon in emotional Cancer doesn't suit
rational Aquarians. You'd rather reason things
out. When the Moon makes its move into fiery
Leo tomorrow, you may want to fight about it.
Don't. You're a natural born thinker.
Sit and think.

With her mustang galloping at full speed, Amber Moyers put the leather reins in her teeth.

"Are you crazy?" shouted her friend Jinx Hubbard, who was riding beside her.

The girls were racing across the New Mexico desert, towards the stables outside Los Alamos where they kept their horses.

Amber threw her arms above her thick, wild, red hair. "I have the power. I have the power," she chanted. Her muscular body rocked in the saddle as the horse pounded ahead.

"Slow down!" Jinx yelled. Although an

experienced rider, she held on to the saddle horn for dear life when her horse had to leap over a tall clump of sagebrush. "Come on, Amber, it's not safe!"

"I have the power," Amber shouted, looping her reins round the saddle horn. Her wire-rimmed glasses bounced up and down on her straight, freckled nose. She closed her eyes and held her palms blissfully upwards towards the sky. She didn't need to look. Behind her closed lids, Amber could see where her horse was headed. She knew that a cloudless blue sky was overhead and the expanse of red desert lay in front of her. "Nothing can harm me," she murmured.

"Amber! Open your eyes!" Jinx pleaded over the thundering hooves. "You're going to hurt yourself!"

"Don't be such a wimp!" Amber shot back, her eyes still closed.

Jinx hunched forwards over the neck of her palomino, Sergeant, trying to keep up with Amber. Her short brown hair, cut in a pageboy, blew away from her face, and the wind made tears form in her big brown eyes.

"Now for trick number two." Amber put all her weight on her left leg and kicked her right leg out of the stirrup. "Look, ma!" she shouted, posing in an arabesque as she galloped along the desert. "I'm dancing!"

"Easy for you," Jinx muttered as she pulled back on the reins to slow Sergeant down. She put all her weight in the left stirrup and slowly raised her right leg behind her. Sergeant continued on his steady path beneath her.

Amber peered over her shoulder at Jinx and grinned. "All right, cowgirl!"

Jinx quickly slid her foot back in the stirrup. "I did it. Are you satisfied? Now let's slow down. Come on, Amber. You're pushing your luck here."

"I like pushing it," Amber giggled. "Now watch this?" In a flash Amber had reversed her position, so she was now facing backwards.

"You are out of your mind!" Jinx cried as the girls cantered side by side.

They'd reached the foot of the mesa. The stables lay just on the other side. Amber knew it without looking. She quickly spun back round and said, "We're almost back. We'd better cool down the horses."

"Right," Jinx agreed.

Amber's feet found the stirrups. Then she unlooped the reins from the horn. "Whoa! Easy now, Riley," she whispered, stroking her horse's neck. Gradually she pulled back on the reins.

Riley responded by slowing from a canter to a trot, then to a walk. Jinx made her palomino do the same.

"That was great!" Amber said. "God, I love the desert!"

"Me, too!" Jinx smiled, revealing the tiny gap between her front teeth. "We're so lucky to live here."

Back at the Double R stables, the girls guided the horses back to the path leading to the corral and the barn. The path crossed through a stand of stunted piñon trees and shrub oak. A small herd of Texas longhorns was grazing a field of thin, pale grass.

"So," Jinx said, "we've been riding for an entire hour and you haven't once mentioned Chris."

Amber turned to look at her friend. "Chris who?"

"What do you mean, Chris who?" Jinx's jaw dropped open. "Don't tell me you two are having problems?"

Amber shook her thick red hair off her shoulders and stared off into the distance. "You might say that."

"But you guys are made for each other!" Jinx insisted. "You're an Aquarius and Chris is an Aries – the stars say that is a great team!"

"Well, maybe the stars are wrong," Amber replied. It had been a whole week since Christopher called a halt to their relationship, but Amber hadn't said a word about it to anyone. Not even to Jinx, her best friend. It was just too painful to discuss.

The girls came out of the trees. The arena was in clear view just ahead. It was a large one, so most of the kids from school practised rodeo events there. In the corral next to the barn, they could see some other riders saddling their horses.

Suddenly Amber jerked her horse to a halt. *Christopher.*

He stood by the rail in all his golden-haired, green-eyed glory, saddling his horse, Winchester. Chris wore his usual tight faded jeans, loose-fitting white T-shirt, and the straw cowboy hat that he and Amber had bought on a day trip to Juarez, Mexico.

"Amber? What's the matter?" Jinx asked, tugging at Sergeant's reins.

She couldn't answer. Amber was gripped by

a tight, dark knot inside her. Something she had only felt a few times in her life. A knot that caused her to twist her head in pain.

"Amber!" Jinx saw the look and reached out to touch her arm. "Are you OK?"

"I don't want to see him," Amber said in a pained whisper.

"See who?"

Amber was barely able to point at Chris, the knot inside her was so intense. "Let's turn back."

"Turn back?" echoed Jinx. "Now? My parents will kill me if I'm late coming home."

"Please, Jinx."

"Amber, what's the big deal?" insisted Jinx. "If you guys are having problems, this is a great chance to talk to him."

"But Chris and I..." Amber started to explain but had to stop.

"Amber, what happened?" prodded Jinx.

"Chris and I are finished," Amber said, fighting to keep the tears from springing to her eyes. "We broke up."

"No way!" Jinx protested. "You two have been together since tenth grade! You're perfect for each other. You both love horses, the desert. Your parents are all scientists—"

"Chris and I are history," Amber interrupted. "He made that very clear."

"When?" Jinx looked as if she was in shock.

"Just a few days ago. It was horrible," admitted Amber. "He said he couldn't see me any more. He just couldn't handle it." Amber threw her arms out to the side. "Handle what?"

Jinx's eyes widened and she whispered out of the side of her mouth, "Don't look now – but Chris is looking this way."

Amber froze. "What should I do?"

"Wave." Jinx plastered a wide grin on her lips. "Look like you're having a great time."

Amber forced herself to smile. She raised her right arm mechanically and flapped her hand. Chris saw her and tipped his hat.

"He looks happy to see you," Jinx murmured. "I think you should go and talk to him."

"Now?"

"No, next year," Jinx said sarcastically. "Of course now."

"Maybe you're right." Amber gently kicked her horse, urging Riley forward. Slowly the girls approached the corral.

"Hi, Amber," Chris said, flashing his winning smile. "Hey, Jinx," he said, nodding in

13

her direction. "Great day for a ride."

"You going off by yourself?" Jinx asked, leaning with her wrists crossed on her saddle horn.

Amber shot Jinx a "cut-it-out" look. She knew what Jinx was doing. Jinx was not so subtly suggesting that Chris invite Amber along.

"Actually," Chris said, kicking at the dirt by the fence with the toe of his boot, "I'm, uh, here with someone."

"Who?" Amber turned in the saddle to look for Chris's riding buddies. They usually could be found hanging out by the Coke machine, or perched on the corral fence, telling not-very-funny jokes. "Brad? Tory?"

"No," Chris said, clearing his throat. He couldn't seem to look Amber in the eye. "Actually, it's—"

"Chris, are you ready?" an unfamiliar female voice called.

Amber turned to see a cute blonde approaching on horseback. The girl's long silken hair was pulled into a ponytail, partially hidden under a black riding helmet. She wore skin-tight black jeans, expensive snakeskin boots, and a yellow halter top that matched her hair colour.

"Amber, Jinx, this is Emily," Chris said. He was very self-conscious. "Amber and Jinx are friends from my school," he explained to the pretty girl.

A friend from school? Amber could feel the dark knot inside her twist.

"Hi." Emily greeted them with a smile that revealed a dimple in each cheek. She turned and looked at Chris adoringly. "We'd better get going before it gets too late."

"Yes, Chris," said Amber between her clenched jaws. "Better go before it's too late."

Chris nodded sheepishly. He placed a boot in the stirrup, grabbed the saddle horn, and hoisted himself into the saddle. "Well, see you guys round, I guess," he said, as he and Emily trotted towards the bridle path.

Amber watched, stunned. Her face stung with embarrassment, as if she'd been slapped. "Some friends from his school?" she repeated his awful words. "That's all he thinks I am?"

Jinx was as shocked as Amber. "I can't believe that guy. When did you say you two broke up?"

"Just a few days ago." Amber's eyes narrowed. "He certainly wasted no time finding

15

my replacement."

"I thought Chris was one of the nice ones," Jinx said, shaking her head. "But he's right up there with the King of the Jerks."

"Come on." Amber pulled on the reins, turning Riley towards the stables. "Let's get out of here."

The girls dismounted and led their horses into the barn. Experienced hands, they removed the bridles, saddles, blankets and then curried and brushed down the horses' sweaty coats.

"I'm sorry," Jinx finally murmured. "About Chris. But don't worry, you'll find someone better."

"I don't want anyone better," Amber replied in an angry voice. "In fact I hate every boy in this town. No, make that every boy on this planet."

Jinx was a little startled by the vehemence of Amber's reply. In typical Jinx fashion, she tried to make a joke of it. "Look on the bright side. Now you'll have more time for doing your nails and working on really fun things like homework."

"Yeah." Amber placed her cheek against Riley's velvet muzzle and sighed. She rummaged in her pocket for a carrot and fed it to him. "Actually, now that you mention it, my science project is going to take a lot of time."

"Why? Isn't that what your parents are for?" asked Jinx with a wink. "I mean, if both of my parents were scientific geniuses, I'd have them do my project."

"Oh, Mom and Dad will help," Amber said, stroking Riley's neck. "I just don't know if they'll approve of my topic."

"Really? What is it?"

"Telekinesis," answered Amber.

"Tele-what?"

"Telekinesis. The ability to move objects with your mind," Amber explained.

"Oh, I saw that guy on TV," Jinx said with a nod. "That guy who can bend spoons and stop watches."

"Uri Geller," Amber said. "I just read a book about him. He really is incredible. At the age of three he could tell his mom exactly how much she had won or lost at cards. At the age of seven he discovered he could cause the hands of his wristwatch to jump ahead to a different hour. And later he discovered he could even bend the watch's hands. When he was twenty-one he was able to have someone draw a picture in another room and he could copy it exactly. I think, if I remember it right, that's when he started bending keys and spoons."

"Whoa!" Jinx shook her head. "I wish I could do that. You know, lie in bed and just think about washing the dishes and they'd be done. Speaking of which..." Jinx checked her watch. "I promised my parents I'd be home in time for dinner. We'd better get a move on."

The girls hurried to Amber's old red pick-up. It needed a new exhaust, the clutch was loose, its fuel consumption was horrendous – but it was Amber's very own. She loved to take the truck off-road in the desert, especially at night when the stars filled the sky.

Amber backed the pick-up away from the corral and drove down the dusty ranch road leading to the highway. "Telekinesis may not be the most successful project, but I think it will be fun to research," Amber said. "I've always been fascinated by what the mind can really do."

"Oh, come on, Amber," Jinx said sceptically. "Don't you think that telekinesis business is a hoax?"

"To tell you the truth, I'm not sure," said Amber, pushing her mass of red hair away from her face. "That's one of the things I'm trying to establish with my research. But you have to admit, Jinx, there's plenty about the universe we don't understand."

"Like guys!" Jinx said, as a car packed full of boys zoomed past them in a cloud of dust. The radio was blasting and the boys were all screaming and waving.

Amber rolled her eyes at Jinx. "Like guys is right." She pulled out on to the highway heading into Los Alamos. "But seriously," Amber continued, "New Mexico is the perfect place to research the paranormal. Look at all of the New Age groups moving into the state."

Jinx shrugged. "I know a lot of locals consider the desert and mountains sacred places of power."

"What about Los Alamos?" Amber gestured towards the town in the distance. "It was right here that scientists unlocked the power of the atom."

"Yeah – so they could make the first atomic bomb," Jinx said ironically.

"OK, some power is better left alone," Amber replied. "But at least consider that I'm on to something."

"You're a regular Aladdin rubbing the magic lamp," Jinx said, laughing at Amber.

After dropping Jinx at her home, Amber pulled her red truck up the driveway of her parents' rambling adobe house on the outskirts of Los Alamos. The front yard consisted of dried grasses and flowers, and a large saguaro cactus.

As Amber came up the walk to the front door, she could hear her parents taking a break from work to play a violin and cello duet. Amber recognized the piece, a rondo by one of her favourite composers, Scarlatti.

Her parents worked at home in separate laboratories at the back of the house. Their idea of relaxation was to play chamber music.

Amber popped her head into the sun room, which was packed with potted cacti and other succulent plants, and called, "I'm home."

"Ah, Amber," her father said, his chin still resting against his violin. "Care to join us?"

"Please do," her mother said, stroking the bow against the strings of her instrument. "Dad rearranged a trio by C.P.E. Bach. We could all move to the piano."

"Not tonight, thanks," Amber said. "I have at least two hours of homework ahead of me. What's for dinner?"

"Dinner?" Her mother repeated the word as

20

if she had never heard it before.

"Dinner," her father explained. "The evening repast that will fortify us for another night's worth of work!"

"Forget it." Amber could tell she was getting nowhere. "I'll order a pizza for us later."

Once in her room, which was decorated with astrological posters and enlarged photographs of the desert, Amber sat down on the side of her bed and pulled off her boots. The odour rising from her socks made her wince – not that she bothered to change them.

A scratching sound at the door let Amber know that her old golden retriever Patsy wanted to come in. Amber pulled the door open and the dog wandered in.

"Hey, Patsy," Amber said, scratching the dog's ears. "How's fleas?"

Patsy wasn't Amber's only pet. On her chest of drawers were two glass aquariums. But instead of being filled with water and tropical fish, one held a horned toad and the smaller one housed Amber's pet tarantula. Above the chest were shelves laden with books, Hopi pottery, and various objects – pieces of a buffalo skull, petrified wood, snakeskin, geodes – that Amber had collected from the desert.

Patsy leapt on Amber's bed, which had a hand-carved pine frame.

"Patsy! Down!"

The dog looked wounded and jumped off. She curled herself up at the foot of the bed on an old Navajo rug. "Now, don't bother me," Amber scolded. "I have homework to agonize over."

At her desk she pushed aside an astrology book and got out her science folder. She thumbed through the articles about telekinesis that she had found at the library, then glanced at a biography about Uri Geller.

The mind was so mysterious. Could a person somehow concentrate all that awesome power and actually affect matter?

With her parents busily playing music in the other room, Amber opened her desk drawer. She took out a spoon that she had borrowed from the kitchen.

Patsy looked up.

"Sorry, girl," Amber said. "This doesn't involve food."

The dog lowered her head again.

Amber cleared an area and placed the spoon down. She stared and stared at it.

"Come on," she whispered. "Bend! Bend!"

She thought of nothing but bending that spoon. In her mind she pictured the metal flexing, the handle folding.

But nothing happened.

"What if this *is* a hoax!" she moaned. "I'm going to have a pretty short science project."

Frustrated, she cleared the top of her desk with a sweep of her hand, sending her folder, books, and the spoon, crashing to the floor, and Patsy fleeing from the room.

Amber stomped to her bed and flopped down on her back. Above the headboard was her bulletin board, crowded with photos, cartoons and other mementos.

She glanced up. There, thumbtacked to the cork, was a photo of Christopher and her, taken only a few weeks before at the stables. They were on horseback and looked very happy together.

Sitting up, she studied the photo. Maybe it held a clue as to why Chris had dumped her so unceremoniously.

"Why?" she whispered. "What did I ever do?"

Now he was with that new girl, Emily. And Amber was home with her lovable, but eccentric parents. Alone.

"I hate you," she told his photo.

Furious, she turned away and stared at the floor. Her gaze wandered across the mess until it finally came to rest on the spoon.

"I hate you, you little worm," she muttered, staring at the spoon. Her eyes began to water – but still she didn't break focus. She stared at the spoon, boring inside it with her mind.

She imagined herself as a powerful probe, going further and further into the metal. In her mind she broke apart its molecules. She split its atoms.

"Get a hold of yourself!" she heard a voice inside her say. The voice caused Amber to blink. Her eyesight went blurry for a moment. She took a breath and let it out slowly. She felt both drained and strangely energized.

But stranger still was the spoon.

"Oh my god!" Amber muttered. She reached down and picked it up.

The handle was bent at a ninety-degree angle.

CHAPTER TWO

The tension is so thick you could cut it with a knife. But you're doing it to yourself, Aquarius. Back off; you're letting your emotions control you.

At lunch the next day, Amber tried to avoid Elena Garcia. Not because they weren't friends. They were. But because, as pep club treasurer, Elena was always trying to get Amber to buy something. Today Elena clutched a handful of tickets in one hand and a metal cash-box in the other.

Keeping her head down, Amber carried her tray with a burger and fries out of the cafeteria to the picnic tables on the quad. It was a glorious spring day. The manzanita trees planted by the school were in blossom, and golden California poppies lined the sidewalks.

"Amber Moyers!" she heard Elena call. "I know you saw me!"

Amber stopped and grinned. She watched Elena, who was one of the most striking girls at Los Alamos West High, stride across the quad. Elena was not just attractive, but flashy. Today she was wearing a bright red-and-green San Antonio Spurs T-shirt, red cycle shorts, and red sandals. Elena liked to tease and spray her fringe so it stood straight up, and wear candy-apple-red lipstick with matching earrings. She was the first to admit, with a gleaming smile: I like to be noticed.

"OK, Elena, you got me," Amber said with a sigh. "What are you selling this time?"

"The Spring All-Conference Rodeo tickets," Elena said, showing a stack to Amber.

"How much?" Amber asked.

"Only five dollars," Elena said. "Seven if you wait and buy one at the gate. Come on, Amber, help me out. If I sell the most, I get three free CDs."

"Here, hold this." Amber handed Elena her tray so she could dig in her bag for a crumpled five-dollar bill. "But first you have to promise not to ask me for any more money for the rest of the week."

Elena shook her head with a grin. "No promises. After all, it's only Monday. Have you seen Kayla or Lori?"

"Your next victims?" Amber asked, taking her tray back. "They're probably holding a table for us."

The girls surveyed the metal picnic tables where many of the students at Los Alamos West High liked to eat their lunch. It allowed them the chance to socialize and work on their tans at the same time.

"There!" Elena said, running ahead. "I'll save you a place."

Amber took her time walking over. She wanted to see her friends, but she was worried that her break-up with Chris would be this lunchtime's main topic of conversation.

"Hey, girlfriend!" Kayla Jackson waved from the centre of the group. She was a stout black girl who wore her hair in a series of corn-row plaits, each ending in a bright plastic bead. When Kayla shook her head it sounded like a clatter of marbles. "What's happening?"

"It seems like it's time for Elena's weekly squeeze," Amber said, taking a seat next to Kayla. "I've already handed over five dollars and it's barely noon."

"Five dollars," Kayla replied. "She hit me for seven. Five for the rodeo and two for a stale old chocolate bar."

"You're not going to eat it?"

Kayla slapped Amber on the shoulder playfully. "Of course I'm going to eat it. But first I'm going to complain about it."

Amber chuckled. "You've always been a sucker for chocolate."

She and Kayla had been friends since second grade. Ever since Kayla's father, a former college football player and now a PhD physicist, had joined Amber's parents and the rest of the staff at the Los Alamos Scientific Laboratory, which was just a few miles from the high school.

"I'll eat what you can't choke down," Jinx called from the end of the table. She was in the process of handing money she had taken from her jeans pocket to Elena, who was smiling triumphantly. She had obviously scored another rodeo ticket sale.

Four of them were seated at the lunch table — Jinx, Elena, Kayla and Amber. Only one person was missing from their group. "Where's Lori?" asked Amber.

"Probably hanging out in the bathroom," Jinx replied with a shake of the head. "That girl had better start taking care of her health."

"She's skipping lunch?" Amber frowned. "Again?"

Kayla nodded. "If she gets any skinnier, we'll be able to use her for a Hallowe'en skeleton."

Jinx took a bite of the cheese sandwich that she'd brought to school. "It's Brad. When is she going to forget about him? It's making her sick!"

Kayla dug her spoon into her carton of cottage cheese. "It's been almost a year since they broke up, and Lori's still moping over that sorry excuse for a boy. When's she going to figure out that he just isn't worth it?"

Jinx pounded her fist on the table. "No boy is. She should just get over him."

"Easy for you to say," Amber said, thinking about Chris.

"Well, Joe knows I'd never forgive him if he ever dropped me for another girl," Elena said. She and Joe had been going out since seventh grade. Everyone assumed they'd probably get married someday.

"You ask me and I'll tell you this," Kayla said, raising her spoon. "Boys can't hold a candle to acting in a play."

"So you're trying out for *Sweeney Todd*?"

asked Jinx, eating the last of her cheese sandwich and corn chips.

"I want to play Mrs Lovett, the crazy pie-maker," Kayla told everyone. "*If* Marnee Moziman doesn't beat me to the part."

"You can sing and act circles round Marnee," said Amber. She loaded some French fries with ketchup before devouring them in one mouthful.

"If only you were directing the musical," Kayla said, swiping one of Amber's fries and popping it in her mouth. "Unfortunately, Ms Whittle's in charge."

"What's the worry?" asked Elena. "Whittle can recognize talent, can't she?"

"Marnie's been sucking up to Ms Whittle big time," Kayla said. "You know Ms Whittle – she always casts her favourite students. And Marnie's all but polishing her hubcaps on a daily basis!"

The image caused the other girls to laugh. However, their good mood was broken when Lori approached.

Lori looked like the poster child for despair. Her long pale-blonde hair was thin and dull. The tip of her nose was always red – she had a permanent note from her allergist which excused her from gym. And her frail shoulders were bent in a perpetual slump. The only time she seemed to brighten up was when she was with Amber and the other girls.

Amber was concerned about Lori's pallor. "Lori, you look a little ill. Why don't I get you a glass of orange juice or something?"

"I just saw Kristal Taylor draped all over Brad," Lori said, fighting back her tears. "It's bad enough that Kristal stole him from me. But does she have to flaunt it every time I see them together?"

"Look, girlfriend," Kayla declared, standing up and giving Lori a hug, "you need to show that boy you can have a good time without him. And you can start by getting some food in you."

"I know," Lori said weakly. She sat down and forced herself to nibble on the apple that Jinx handed her.

"Lori, I know you're having a bad day." Elena held up her tickets. "But the rodeo's coming up and—"

"Stop," Lori said, unzipping her bumbag. She reached in and took out a handful of carefully folded dollar bills. "Five dollars, right?" She handed the money to Elena.

Elena gave Lori a sympathetic smile.

"Thanks, Lori." Then she turned to Kayla. "That's four tickets sold. You're the only hold-out."

Kayla rolled her eyes. "Oh, puh-leeze. You know I don't go for all of that horse business."

Elena put one hand on her hip and continued to stare at Kayla. "Come on, where's your school spirit? I go to see your plays!"

"OK! OK!" Kayla threw her hands in the air. "Take my last five dollars – go ahead!"

Elena took it without a second thought.

"But, if LA West doesn't end up in first place," Kayla said, narrowing her eyes at Elena, "I want my money back."

"We'll win," Elena said, locking her cash-box. "Troy Evans is the reigning barrel racing champ. And Christopher's calf-roping is getting better all the time. Isn't that right, Amber?"

Amber nodded and muttered darkly, "You should see the heifer he was roping yesterday at the ranch."

"You should enter." Jinx pointed her sandwich at Amber. "You're a great rider. You'd probably win the girl's barrel racing."

"No thanks," Amber said. "I love to ride. But rodeos are cruel to animals."

"Barrel racing is cruel?" Jinx squinted one eye shut and peered at Amber.

"Can we drop it?" Amber said with an edge. The idea of being on a team or even near any arena with Christopher upset her.

At the next table, one of their classmates, Doug Farber, dumped the remains of his lunch in the trash. He was a really nice guy and one of the girls' pals, so it wasn't unusual when he wandered over. "So, what are the Gang of Five plotting today?" he asked with a grin.

"The takeover of LA West," Kayla said, rubbing her hands in front of her and talking like a witch. "Today, the high school — tomorrow, the world." Kayla threw her head back and did a full-throated mad scientist cackle that made everyone laugh.

"If your takeover is successful," Doug said, focusing on Jinx, "put me down for one of your love slaves."

Jinx blushed and Kayla jabbed her with her elbow.

Elena, never one to let an opportunity pass, raised her tickets. "Yo, Doug—"

"Whoa!" Doug pulled out the pockets of his trousers to show Elena he had no money. "I'm cleaned out."

"Where's your school spirit?" Elena said, pouting.

"I'm sorry, Elena. I'm a terrible human being." Doug dramatically flung one arm to his forehead. "I should be flogged. Better yet, hogtied and dragged across the rodeo arena." He flopped backwards on the table in front of Jinx and then raised himself up on one elbow. "So, Jinxie, what say we hit the desert this afternoon and work on our project?"

Jinx laughed so hard that yogurt spurted out of her mouth, which caused everyone to hoot with laughter and Jinx to turn a bright shade of red.

"Jinxie?" Amber arched an eyebrow.

"We're using Geiger counters to see if there's any excess radioactivity present in the desert," Doug explained. "Due to all of the nuclear research done at the lab."

"Don't overlook those abandoned uranium mines up in the hills," Elena reminded them.

Doug nodded. "The ghost towns. Thanks."

"I'm not going to any of those ghost towns," Jinx declared with a shudder.

"You'll be safe with me," Doug assured her.

"So you two have gone off into the desert before?" Amber asked with a mischievous grin.

34

"A few times." Jinx defiantly folded her arms and stared hard at Amber. "Any law against it?"

"You and Doug, alone in the desert," Amber continued, just to torture Jinx. "Conducting *research*."

"Yes, research," Jinx practically shouted.

"Uh-oh." Doug peeled himself off the table and stood up. "Looks like there's gonna be shoutin'," he drawled. "That's my cue to vamoose." Doug backed away with a wave. "I'll call you later, Jinxie."

As soon as he left, the girls zeroed in on Jinx. "*Jinxie?*"

"All right, girlfriend, confess!" Kayla said.

"You and Doug Farber!" Elena gasped.

"I thought you were too busy for boys," Amber teased.

"Lay off her," Lori cut in. "Doug's a great guy."

"Yeah, leave me alone!" insisted Jinx, her face turning a brighter shade of crimson. "Doug and I are just friends."

"Friends who happen to drive out to the desert to conduct research daily," teased Amber.

"You're just jealous!" accused Jinx.

"Me?" Amber scoffed. "Jealous? Of what?"

"Because a boy is showing an interest in me, and you and Chris—"

"Jinx..." Amber shot her a warning look.

But it was too late.

"You and Chris – what?" demanded Lori.

Amber threw her hands in the air. "Thanks a lot, Jinx!"

But she knew it was going to come out sooner or later. Amber took a deep breath and faced her friends. "Chris and I broke up."

For a moment the others were shocked speechless.

"You're joking," Elena gasped finally.

"I wish," Amber said, lowering her eyes.

"But – but why?" whispered Kayla.

"He won't tell me," Amber said. "I think it's because he met this new girl – Emily – at the stables."

"Oh, Amber." Lori, with watery blue eyes, reached out and touched Amber's hand. "I'm so sorry."

"It's no big deal," Amber tried to bluff. "I realized that there were a lot more important things in life than Chris. I don't have time for him anyway. At least not now. What with working on my science project and all."

"Science project?" Kayla hit her head with the palm of her hand. "I haven't even started mine. What are you doing — that thing about gravity?"

Amber shook her head. She was still thinking about Chris and it was hard to change her focus.

"She's doing one on tele-kinkiness," Jinx joked, jabbing Amber with her elbow.

"Telekinesis," Amber corrected.

"You mean moving things round the room just by thinking about them?" Lori asked. "That only works in the movies."

"No, I did it in my room," Amber said quietly. "I bent a spoon with my mind."

The other girls looked at one another. They weren't sure if Amber was serious or joking.

"You bent a spoon?" repeated Kayla.

"That's right," Amber said.

"Just by thinking about it?" added Elena.

Amber nodded. "I got so mad at seeing Chris with that Emily girl at the ranch that I focused my anger on a spoon. And bent it."

"Whoa!" Kayla snorted.

"That is *major* weird," added Elena.

"I swear it happened," said Amber.

Jinx wiped her yogurt spoon clean with a

paper napkin. Then she placed it in front of Amber. "OK. Show us."

"Fine." Amber stared at the spoon. She tried to focus all of her mental energy – but it wasn't easy with her friends watching. After a minute she gave up. "I can't concentrate right now. I think it only works when there's a real focus of power. Maybe all of us should try it."

"No way," Elena said, glancing over her shoulder. "I can't think with all these people round."

"Me neither," added Lori. "Besides, people think I'm weird enough already."

"Well, maybe we should get together after school," Amber suggested. She thought for a moment, then said, "I know! I'll ask my parents if we can have a slumber party at my house on Friday."

"Cool," said Elena. "I'll tell Joe he can only see me on Saturday night so he better think of something fun."

"I have a Ouija board I can bring over," volunteered Lori.

"And we can do each other's horoscopes," added Amber. "I know a little bit about astrology, and so does Jinx."

"Oo-oo!" Kayla wiggled her fingers in the

38

air. "An occult slumber party. I love it. We can even dress up for the occasion!"

"I have a perfect gypsy outfit," Elena said, enthusiastically. "It's got lots of jewellery and a really fun skirt made of scarves."

"Jinx, are you in?" Amber asked. "Or do you and Doug have some research you need to do?"

"I'm in," Jinx said. Then she mumbled into her shoulder, "And, listen, I'm sorry I blabbed about you and Chris."

"It's all right," Amber assured her. "It had to come out sometime."

"All right!" Elena pumped her fist in the air. "Slumber party. Friday. Be there, or be square."

"We can get all weird and occult," Kayla intoned. "And try to warp the Moyers' silverware."

"Kayla, you're already warped!" Jinx chuckled.

The bell rang and the girls got ready for the start of afternoon class. Before going their separate ways, they promised to call each other that night and finalize plans for the slumber party.

Amber was feeling better as she carried her tray towards the trash. She had something fun to look forward to. *Who needs Chris?*

39

Then she saw him talking to his buddies. Chris noticed her, too, but pretended he hadn't seen her. He deliberately turned his back as she walked by.

Remembering how much he had hurt her, Amber felt that dark knot in the back of her mind surface again.

You're going to get what you deserve. You can't treat me like that.

"Amber, better hurry to class," Jinx called, but Amber didn't hear her.

Instead she focused on the dark knot of anger.

Reaching the trash bin, she lifted her tray — and it flew out of her hands at an alarming speed. It hit the container with such force that it knocked it over. Trash scattered across the ground, and everyone stopped to watch.

Amber was stunned. *Did I do that?* She reached down and righted the bin. *Could I really have the power to propel things?*

Horrified, she quickly stuffed the trash back inside the trash bin and raced past Chris to her next class.

CHAPTER THREE

There is something crackling in the air —
change. Whether it's for better or worse, is up
to you.

On Friday evening the unpredictable spring
weather seemed to know that Amber was
hosting an occult slumber party. The night was
eerily dark, with the moon and stars masked by
black, ominous clouds. Lightning thunder, and
rain had begun right after dinner and hadn't
slowed by the time the girls arrived.

Thanks to Kayla, each girl came in a
costume borrowed from the drama department
collection. Amber was dressed like a gypsy
palm reader, a red scarf tied round her head and
bracelets clanking on her wrists.

"Where are your parents?" Jinx asked,
tossing her sleeping bag on to the living room
floor. She was dressed as a sorceress in a long,
pale-blue chiffon gown. Round her neck she

wore an amulet attached to a silk ribbon.

"Gone for the night," answered Amber. "They went into Santa Fe to the opera, and are staying over at some bed-and-breakfast place they like."

"I can't imagine my parents ever doing anything romantic like that." Elena wrinkled her nose. She wore a witch's black cape and had painted her fingernails to match. "It would be too gross."

Amber shrugged. "My folks take romantic trips all the time."

"So the house is all ours?" Jinx asked with a devilish grin.

"The house is my responsibility," Amber said firmly. "Which means no raiding the liquor cabinet, no going through my parents' things, no extra loud music, no—"

"OK, OK," Kayla said, stopping her. "We get the point. Let me ask one thing – we *can* have a good time, right?"

Amber chuckled. "Of course.

"You're lucky. *My* parents don't trust me any further than they can throw me," Lori sniffed. She wore a fringed scarf tied round her waist which partly covered her black leggings, and a peasant blouse. "I practically had to sign a pledge to stay out of trouble tonight. And I had to change into this in the car, or they never would've let me come."

"Tell me about it," Elena said. "My mother, self-appointed protector of the Catholic church, made me swear not to have anything to do with the devil's work."

Kayla laughed. "My mom's happy I'm gone for the night. Dad, as usual stayed late at the lab, so Mom said she's going out with her girlfriends."

The girls stowed their sleeping bags with Jinx's in the living room. Then Amber brought out a tray full of pizza bagels, a bowl of freshly popped corn, blue tortilla chips and salsa, and some big bottles of mineral water. While everyone helped themselves, Amber got out her book on astrology.

"I looked up the signs of everyone here. But I'm not going to tell you what they are. You have to guess who's what after I read the description."

"I like guessing games," Elena said, sitting cross-legged on the floor by the coffee table.

"OK, here's the first one." Amber opened the book to a slip of paper she'd tucked inside it. "'Friendships are very important to her. But she can be insecure and moody, getting her feelings hurt over the least little thing one second, and bouncing back the next.'"

"Piece of cake," Kayla declared. "You're describing Lori to a T!"

Amber touched her nose. "Bingo. Lori's our Gemini."

"Am I really that wishy-washy?" Lori groaned.

"Only on really bad days," Jinx said, trying to make her feel better.

"Do another one," urged Elena.

Amber flipped to another section of the book. "'High-spirited and proud. Extremely trustworthy, she makes and keeps friends easily. She loves outdoor sports, especially where dogs and horses are—'"

"Me!" interrupted Jinx. "You're describing Sagittarius, which is my sun sign."

"Very good," Amber grinned. "OK, here's number three. 'A fiery personality. Where others cringe from the challenge, she charges full steam ahead. She craves the spotlight and will do anything to hold centre stage, but her generous energy makes everyone forgive her.'"

All eyes turned to Kayla. She blushed, a little. "OK, you got me nailed, I'm a Leo," she said to Amber. "We all want to be on stage!"

"That leaves Amber and me," said Elena.

"So guess who I'm describing," Amber said, turning to another section in the book. "'She's the material girl. She's incredibly stubborn, particularly when seeking the financial advantage—'"

"Elena!" the girls shouted in unison before bursting into laughter.

"It's weird how accurate astrology can be," Lori said, tucking a strand of her hair behind one ear. "Do you think we really do reflect our sun signs, or did you just pick out what you knew to be our characteristics?"

"Let's see that." Kayla snatched the book out of Amber's hands. "I'll read the opening paragraph that describes our resident Aquarius."

"Wait a minute." Amber tried to grab the book back but Kayla held it out of reach.

"Ah-ah-ah," Kayla said. "Turnabout is fair play, remember?"

"OK," Amber agreed reluctantly.

"Here we are," Kayla continued, finding the right chapter. "'She is noble, moderate and sound. Even though she is the most peace-loving of signs, this eccentric girl ends up in unpredictable situations. She is scientific, loves new inventions and mysteries, especially those having to do with psychic research.'"

"Yep, that's our Amber," Elena said, dipping a corn chip into the fresh salsa.

Amber took her notepad and under the heading Astrology made several notations. "So, in our small group, we could probably say that, at least on the surface, astrology seems to work. I guess if we were really to get into it, we'd have to know everyone's time of birth and then we'd do their chart, finding out what's their moon sign and where all their planets were at the moment they were born."

Jinx paused with a chip halfway to her mouth. "We're going to do all that? I thought we were going to do the Ouija board."

Amber chuckled. "Don't worry, that's next. You did bring it, didn't you, Lori?"

As Lori nodded, Elena shivered. "Just thinking about it gives me goose bumps."

Kayla's beads clacked together as she nodded emphatically. "Me too."

Amber drew the blinds and lit a few candles before turning off the lights. Shadows bounced across the walls and ceiling, making the night even more eerie.

"Sorry, old girl," Amber told Patsy, pulling the dog by the collar into the other room and locking the door. "But the occult is not for pets."

Returning to the living room, Amber covered the card table with a dark cloth, then set the Ouija board in the center. The girls pulled up chairs and gathered round.

"Now we have to take this seriously," Amber warned the group. "Otherwise, we're just wasting our time."

"Hear that, Kayla?" Lori said. "No pretending to be a fake ghost."

"*Moi*?" Kayla said in mock protest.

Each of the girls gently placed her fingertips on the planchette. Then they closed their eyes so they couldn't see the pointer move.

"Let's start with an easy question," Amber advised. "How many people are here tonight?"

The planchette quivered, tugged by the individual energy of each girl. Then it began to slide under its own power. When it stopped, the girls opened their eyes.

"Five!" cried Elena. "It worked!"

"Let me try a question," Kayla insisted. "Who will get cast in *Sweeney Todd* – me or Marnee Moziman?"

47

"Are you sure you want the answer?" asked Lori.

"I'm sure," Kayla said, firmly. She was the first to close her eyes.

The other girls followed suit. Again the planchette shook before gently starting to slide.

The girls opened their eyes.

The planchette first stopped on the letter *M*.

"Maybe it stands for Me," said Kayla hopefully.

But then it moved to *A*, and then *R*.

"That's all I can stand," said Kayla. She pulled her hands away. "I hate that Marnee Moziman. I have more talent in my fingernail than she has in her whole body. I can't believe she'll get the part!"

"Maybe the board's wrong," suggested Jinx.

"I hope so," Kayla muttered.

"I have a question," said Lori. "Will Doug Farber and Jinx fall madly in love?"

"I don't think I want the answer," Jinx said quickly. She crossed her arms, unwilling to participate.

"Come on," Amber said. "Everyone has to help."

The girls placed their fingertips on the planchette. In a matter of moments it moved to the *Y*, the *E*, and the *S*.

"I'm telling you Doug and I are just friends!" Jinx protested. No one believed her.

"I have a question for the board," Lori said, to everyone's surprise. "Will Brad and I ever get back together?"

The girls placed their fingertips on the planchette. Again the pointer slid round the board, spelling out *N O*.

"I guess I already knew that," conceded Lori. "I just had to ask."

"OK, one last question." Jinx placed her fingertips on the pointer. "Oh, great and powerful Ouija board, will Chris get back together with Amber?"

Before the other girls could even touch it, the planchette leapt off the board and skittered across the living room floor.

"Whoa," Kayla breathed. "I'd say that was a definite 'No way!'"

"You did that!" Amber accused Jinx.

"Did not!" Jinx shot back.

"Then someone else did!" Amber glared at the other girls.

Just then candles went out, as if blown by a phantom wind. Yet no windows or doors were open, which meant someone – or something –

inside the living room was responsible.

"Very funny, Lori," Elena said in a shaky voice.

"I didn't blow those candles out," Lori whispered.

"I didn't either," echoed Kayla.

"I'm too far away," Jinx said from the darkness.

"Well, *I* didn't do it," Amber said, a little too loudly.

The girls were suddenly frightened.

"Turn on the light, somebody," Lori pleaded.

Kayla agreed. "Maybe this occult stuff shouldn't be messed with."

"Yeah, maybe we should just make some more popcorn and watch a movie on cable," suggested Jinx.

Amber leapt to her feet and fumbled in the dark for the light switch. She finally found it and turned the living room lights back on.

"Look at my arms," Lori said. "I have a major case of goose bumps!"

"Me, too," said Elena. "I'm totally creeped out!"

The storm outside knocked a tree branch against the window. The girls recoiled from the table and clutched at each other.

"No more Ouija board for me!" Kayla said, grabbing Lori and Elena. "That thing is possessed!"

"Maybe the combination of the five of us tapped into its real power," Amber suggested.

"Right," said Jinx, rolling her eyes. "So now let's bend a few spoons and call it an early night."

"Jinx, nothing will work if you deny even the possibility," said Amber. "I was reading this article about telekinesis and it described a woman whose baby was trapped under a car. This car weighed like a ton. But this panicked mother used adrenalin and telekinesis to lift that car and save her baby."

"I heard something like that, too," Kayla said. "A man hiking got caught in a rock slide. Trapped beneath this boulder and about to die, he used his mind to move it just high enough for him to escape."

"I think if the five of us really concentrate together," Amber said, "we can do anything." Without another word she went to the sideboard in the dining room and took out a spoon.

She passed the spoon round the table. "See if you can bend it with your hands," she challenged.

None of the girls could.

"So we all agree, this spoon is solid metal," Amber said, placing it in the centre of the card table.

The others nodded.

"OK. Everyone think about bending this spoon," Amber said, resuming her seat. "Visualize the metal twisting and bending. Don't allow yourself to think about anything else. Don't look at anyone else. Don't break focus. Concentrate on the task of bending the spoon. Only that."

Each of the girls stared at the spoon. Amber focused her mind like she never had before.

"It's not going to work," Jinx predicted.

"Be quiet!" Amber ordered. "Or leave the room."

"Let's start over," Kayla suggested.

Again the girls focused all their mental energy on the spoon. Ten seconds elapsed, then half a minute.

Then the spoon bent, as easily as a wet piece of spaghetti!

The girls let out a cheer.

"Whoa! We did it!" Amber screamed.

"Weird," Elena cried, clutching her head. "Totally weird!"

"Scary," Lori whispered.

"That wasn't some trick spoon, was it?" Jinx asked, squinting at Amber.

"I swear it wasn't." Amber raised her right hand

"I believe it," Kayla said, dancing round the room. "I can feel the power of the girlfriends!"

"Well, I'm still not convinced," Jinx said.

"Let's try something else, something bigger," Kayla cried. "Come on, Jinx, you pick it."

"All right." Jinx looked round the room. "Let's levitate the coffee table."

"Couldn't we try something smaller?" Lori asked. "Like a lamp or an ashtray."

"No, Jinx is right," Amber said. "If we truly have the power, the size of an object shouldn't matter."

"Let's all hold hands so no one can be accused of cheating," suggested Kayla.

"Good idea," said Amber. She took Elena and Lori by the hand. "Now really focus all of your energy on the table. But first repeat after me, 'I have the power'."

The other girls joined the circle of hands and repeated, "I have the power."

"The power is strong," Amber said in a clear

firm voice.

"The power is strong."

"Now visualize the table lifting off the floor," Amber directed. "See it being raised higher and higher. It will not fall. It's safely under our power. Really concentrate on the tiny space between the bottom of the table legs and the floor. Now use your minds to widen that space. Wider and wider."

Amber saw between half-closed lids that the coffee table was hovering above the ground!

"Keep going," Amber continued. "I want us to raise this table, which is light as a feather, up to the ceiling. It's light as a feather."

The table gently rose and rose. The girls' fingernails were all digging into each others' hands. They were barely breathing.

"Now, open your eyes – and see!" Amber whispered.

The girls saw the table floating just beneath the ceiling.

"Oh god!" moaned Elena. "I don't believe it!"

"We did it!" Jinx gasped.

"We can do anything!" Kayla chimed in.

Lori started to tremble violently. "I can't hold it any longer!" she cried, pulling her hands free.

Instantly the table crashed to the floor.

"Lori, are you all right?" asked Amber.

"I'm fine," Lori said. "I just got frightened. I mean, I've never believed in...in whatever — other-worldly powers — before tonight."

"Lori, you may be fine," Elena said. "But the Moyers' coffee table is a mess!"

One of the table legs had snapped in two, and a corner was badly chipped. "My parents will kill me!" moaned Amber.

Jinx bent down to examine the broken table. "Don't worry," she said. "It's nothing a few nails and some carpenter's glue won't fix."

Kayla was all smiles as she hugged Amber. "Girlfriend, if we can do that, we can do just about anything."

Amber's heart seemed to be pounding a million times a second in her chest. She knew that Kayla was right. She and her friends had discovered a new and awesome power.

CHAPTER FOUR

Powerful and disruptive vibes are at work because of a bad passage of Saturn. You're still angry about some slight you feel; personal, educational or financial. Sometimes the best course of action is no action.

"Mom? Dad? Can I talk to you about something?"

Her parents had barely unpacked from their overnight trip to Santa Fe. It was early Saturday afternoon and all of Amber's friends had gone home.

"Of course," her mother said. "I'm making some tea. We can talk in the sun room."

"You and your friends didn't break something, did you?" her father asked, peering over his round tortoiseshell glasses.

Amber remembered the coffee table, and the great job she and Jinx had done of repairing it that morning. "Oh, no, Dad," she fibbed.

"Nothing like that."

Her mother brought a tray of tea, fruit, and sandwiches into the sun room. The family sat down, her father Stefan on a wicker chair, Amber and her mother Harriet sharing the wicker sofa with its Indian patterned cushions.

"So, Amber, what's on your mind?" Harriet asked.

"As scientists," Amber began, "do you believe there are some things in this world that are...well, unexplainable?"

Her parents grinned. They greatly enjoyed a good discussion.

"You mean that certain natural processes may elude definition through traditional scientific ratiocination?" her mother asked.

Amber blinked several times. As much time as she spent with her parents, it still took her a few moments to adjust to their "techno-speak", as Kayla called it. "Yeah, that's what I mean."

"Well, there are certainly some phenomena in nature which scientists have yet to fully comprehend, much less explain," Stefan said, sipping his camomile tea thoughtfully. "For example, we don't understand how certain diseases operate. Or why dinosaurs became extinct. Or how the universe began."

"I'm not thinking that big," Amber said. "I'm talking about — I don't know how to explain it — the power of the mind to do things it shouldn't be able to do."

Her parents glanced at each other. Only for a moment, but long enough for Amber to know some troublesome thought had passed between them.

Harriet picked up the plate of vegetarian sandwiches made with her homemade spicy mustard. She held it in front of Amber. "I'm not sure what you're asking. Are you curious about ESP — extrasensory perception?"

"OK, let me try again," Amber told her seemingly befuddled parents. "For my science project I'm doing research on telekinesis."

Her father choked on his sandwich. After dabbing his mouth with a napkin, he said, "Ah. The power of mind over matter. Specifically, when the body generating the force does not come in contact with the object that is affected."

"Well, is it possible?" Amber continued. "Is it possible for the human mind to bend objects, or move them?"

Stefan cleared his throat. "The phenomenon known as telekinesis has neither been proven conclusively, nor has it been demonstrated to be a hoax," he said in his stiff way. "Certainly, experts have proven that we humans use a relatively small percentage of our brainpower – some say as little as five per cent. Even Einstein, they believed, only used twenty to twenty-five per cent of his brain's potential."

"Which means," Harriet added, "that it lies within the realm of possibility for an individual capable of tapping the mind's full potential to possibly – I stress, possibly – affect his or her immediate environment."

"Another thing we can't rule out," said Stefan, "is that some individuals may think they have telekinetic powers – while, in fact, they're just mentally disturbed. In other words, they *think* they see objects moving but it's all a hallucination. Quite literally, in their heads."

"So you're saying telekinesis *is* possible," Amber concluded.

"We're saying it's difficult to know one way or the other," Harriet clarified. "Like most science, the way telekinesis has been treated in books and movies and on television is highly unreliable, scientifically speaking."

"Have you ever dealt with the phenomenon in your own research?" Amber asked.

Since her parents worked at the Los Alamos Scientific Laboratory, the home of the largest linear accelerator, they spent much of their time studying subatomic particles.

Her mother set her teacup in its saucer. "Granted, we do deal with forces of nature, like quarks and mesons, that are so difficult to define as to seem supernatural. So far we can only glimpse any physical evidence that they exist, yet scientists can describe them mathematically with great accuracy. But neither your father nor I have ever actually studied these alleged psychokinetic powers."

"OK," Amber said, "for argument's sake, let's say telekinesis is possible. How would it actually work?"

"Harriet, you're the theoretical physicist," Stefan said to his wife. "So, get theoretical."

Her mother thought for a moment. "Objects affect each other's state of motion all the time," she said. "Newton pointed this out with his laws of motion and gravitation in the late seventeenth century. For instance, the Earth never touches the moon. But the Earth has trapped the moon in its orbit due to the Earth's much larger mass."

"So maybe in telekinesis the mind

concentrates its own energy," Amber said, "as intensely as some mental black hole. And this power allows it to move objects."

"Intriguing postulation," Stefan chuckled. "Very good!"

"But how would you prove it?" Amber asked.

"No one has — yet," Harriet said. "Amber, maybe you'll be the first."

"Mom, I'm a high school senior," Amber said, blushing. "Not a Nobel Prize winner."

"Well, to my knowledge, all Nobel Prize winners were high school seniors once," Stefan joked.

"You two are probably using as much of your brains as Einstein. Have either of you ever felt you had telekinetic powers?" Amber asked.

Her parents glanced at each other again.

"Not I," Stefan said.

"Nor I," Harriet added. "Why?"

Amber was about to tell them about the spoon, about the lunch tray that hurled itself at the trash bin and the coffee table — when Stefan's watch began to beep.

"That's my signal," he said, standing up. Having to spend so many hours bent over his desk, he'd developed a bad back. Now he made sure to stand up at least once an hour, whether he was working or not.

The beep set off an alarm in Amber's head. "Dad, what time is it?"

Stefan glanced at his watch. "Two forty-eight and...sixteen seconds."

"Oh, no!" Amber said getting to her feet. "I told Jinx I'd meet her at the stables at two-thirty."

"In that case, we'll continue this discussion some other time," her mother said, dabbing her mouth with her napkin. "Be careful riding."

"Mom, I'm always careful," Amber said with a toss of her head.

At the stables, one of the wranglers told Amber that Jinx had gone on ahead. Amber quickly saddled Riley and raced out to the meadow pretty with spring wild flowers where Jinx usually liked to ride.

Sure enough, she found Jinx putting her horse through a series of tight turns used in competitive barrel racing.

"Amber, where were you?" Jinx asked, reining Sergeant in.

"Talking to my parents," Amber said, stopping her horse near Jinx's palomino.

"Are you in trouble?"

"No," said Amber. "The table looks great. It'll be years before they discover the crack."

"Elena called me twenty minutes after she got home from the slumber party," Jinx said. "She's in major hot water with her mom."

Amber knitted her eyebrows together. "For sleeping over at my house?" she asked.

"Because Elena was stupid enough to tell her mom about the Ouija board," Jinx said. "Her mom blew up. She said the occult was absolutely against their religion. You know she's a major Catholic."

"Poor Elena," said Amber.

"She should've known better," said Jinx without much sympathy. "Here's the kicker. Her mom's so angry that she's banned Elena from seeing any of us."

"What?" gasped Amber. "She can't do that!"

"She thinks she can," Jinx told her.

"Did Elena mention the table-lifting to her mom?" Amber asked.

"Are you crazy?" Jinx said. "At least she had the sense not to bring that up. If her mom got that freaked about a Ouija board, imagine what she'd do about the table-lifting — have us burned as witches!"

63

"It's important we keep this just between us," Amber declared. "Otherwise people will think we're weird."

"Yeah," Jinx said, removing her cowboy hat and pushing back her short brown hair. "We've always walked the weird line as it is. This would send us into the no-return zone."

"I think we need to have a meeting right away," Amber said, pursing her lips. "Tonight!"

Jinx put her hat back on her head. "Did you hear what I just said? Elena can't see us."

"Well, what about the others?" asked Amber.

"Kayla has plans, I know," Jinx said. "Lori's probably available, like most Saturday nights since she and Brad broke up."

Amber leant forward on the saddle horn. "Do you think you could sneak out late?"

"I can try," Jinx said, swallowing hard. "But remember what happened last time I got caught? I was grounded for a month."

"We just won't get caught," Amber said quietly. "But we definitely need to meet. Let's finish our ride. And when we get home, I'll phone the others."

The girls rode side by side to the top of a low mesa. The afternoon sun felt good, restoring some of their optimism that things would be fine. In fact Amber was feeling excited by the sudden intrigue of sneaking out late. That is, until she spotted Christopher riding in the distance.

He was riding alone cantering through an open expanse dotted with sagebrush.

Watching him, Amber felt that dark knot form inside her brain. The pain was so intense that she had to grab the saddle horn to keep her from falling.

"Amber, are you all right?" asked Jinx.

"I don't know," said Amber, rubbing her head. "Lately I've been getting these horrible shooting pains."

"Maybe you're possessed by the devil," joked Jinx.

"This isn't funny," said Amber. "It isn't normal. It's this thing that doesn't feel like it's a part of me. Like something is crushing my thoughts into a black hole."

"Sometimes I get that feeling in my stomach when I'm hungry," Jinx joked again. "Or when I'm trying to think of an answer in calculus."

Amber was at a loss, not finding a way to describe her black pain accurately. It was like something bad inside her – but she was afraid to tell Jinx that.

Instead she said, "I guess I should be used to it. I've had this feeling lurking inside me for as long as I can remember. Like for sixteen years."

"Even when you were a baby?" Jinx asked.

Amber cocked her head. "Yes, I think even then."

Jinx's eyes widened. "You can actually remember back to when you were a baby? I'm lucky if I can remember anything before my fifth birthday. And then it's mostly Christmas, or when I stepped on a dead frog, or had a really bad fall off my trike."

"Maybe I can remember because I started speaking before my first birthday," Amber said. "My parents say we form our memories in language, so pre-verbal experiences are almost impossible to remember."

"Yeah, that sounds like something your parents would say," Jinx observed facetiously.

"Oh, I could talk up a storm by my second birthday," Amber said as she guided Riley along a sagebrush-lined path that led away from Chris. "Complete sentences, the whole shebang. But – maybe because I was concentrating on talking – I didn't take a step until I was nearly three."

"Wow. Your parents must've freaked!" Jinx

said, trotting up beside her.

Amber nodded. "No kidding."

"What was the matter?" asked Jinx.

"My parents said they took me to lots of doctors, but all they could figure out was I didn't need to walk."

"You didn't need to walk?" Jinx looked perplexed.

"I was able to ask for whatever I needed," Amber explained. "And my parents would bring it to me. The few things I didn't ask for, like toys and pillows and jigsaw puzzles, would seem to magically appear by my side."

"Wait a second," Jinx interrupted. "Things would just appear right near you?"

Amber shrugged her shoulders. "My parents assumed that I was crawling at lightning speed. That, while their backs were turned, I'd gather my toys and blankets and pillows."

Jinx whistled between her teeth. "That's totally weird. I thought you were unusual. But this beats everything."

Amber had never really thought that much about her childhood, but Jinx's reaction made her wonder. Maybe she really was – different.

"This explains why your parents had only one kid," Jinx joked.

Amber swiped at Jinx with her hat and missed.

Jinx dug her heels into Sergeant's sides. "Race you back to the corral!" she bellowed over her shoulder.

The girls took off down the mesa. Jinx had the early lead, but Amber soon came up even with her. As the girls reached the final turn into the ranch, Amber nudged her horse ahead.

"Look, there's Chris!" Jinx shouted from behind Amber.

If Amber could have slammed on the brakes, she would have. She tugged back on Riley's reins. "Whoa, boy. Whoa. Easy now."

Chris was unsaddling Winchester inside the corral. He didn't notice Amber till she was next to him.

"Where's your friend?" Amber challenged.

Chris glared at her. "Emily fell off her horse the last time you saw her and hasn't come back to ride."

Amber was stunned. "You say that as if I had something to do with it."

"I wonder," Chris muttered, lifting the saddle off Winchester's back.

"Oh, come on!" protested Amber dismounting. "I wasn't anywhere near Emily's horse."

Chris waited until Jinx moved out of earshot.

"Amber," he said, "remember our ride to the arroyo?"

"Of course," she said with hurt feelings. "It was our last ride together. What about it?"

"Remember how I wanted to go down to the spring, to the left?" he said. "But you wanted to ride along the ridge."

"So?"

"I suggested we split up and meet back here," he continued. "But suddenly my horse pulled right and no matter what I tried, I couldn't get him to go towards the spring."

"Chris, why are you telling me this story?" Amber asked, putting one hand on her hip.

"I think you know," he said firmly.

"Maybe something to the left spooked Winchester," she suggested. "Maybe it was snake."

Chris shrugged. "Maybe. But I tugged and tugged. Finally, I let him have his way and Chester led me right to you on top of the ridge."

"What are you saying?" Amber shook her head in confusion. "That I put some weird spell on your horse?"

Chris smoothed the ground with the toe of his cowboy boot. "Did you?" he asked without looking up.

"Don't be ridiculous!" Amber huffed. "I'm sorry if you can't control your horse. And I'm sorry if you lost your blonde friend. But believe me, Chris, I had nothing to do with any of that."

"Oh, really." Without another word, Chris took his horse by the reins and led him to the barn.

Amber was left with her mouth hanging open, dumbfounded at his words.

CHAPTER FIVE

*T*hat night, well past her usual bedtime, Amber left her parents a note taped to her pillow:

> Mom & Dad —
> In case you come in here – I had to meet my friends. A couple of them are having personal problems and need to talk. Don't worry! I took my truck and will be back soon. Thanks for trusting me – A.

She had been on the phone to her friends, and all had agreed to a midnight rendezvous. Now she wanted to slip out without having to explain why to her parents. And she needed to do it without Patsy, barking.

Creeping by Patsy's bed in the utility room, Amber whispered, "Good girl. Now stay quiet."

The dog began to wag her tail and stretch,

but Amber was prepared. She reached down and presented Patsy with a favourite treat, cottage cheese and a sliced hot dog, which kept the animal occupied.

Outside, to ensure that she didn't disturb her parents, Amber released the pick-up's parking brake, put it into neutral, and let it roll down the driveway before starting the engine.

Her first stop was Jinx's house. Amber flashed the truck's headlights three times, as arranged. A moment later, she saw Jinx sneaking out of a side door.

"So far, so good," Amber reported as Jinx quietly got in the front seat beside her.

"Take it nice and slow," advised Jinx. "Don't want to wake the neighbours."

"Did you get hold of Lori?" Amber asked.

Jinx nodded. "She has to wait till her parents' lights go out. Her mom likes to watch all the late night TV. So Lori said she'd meet us at the big rock in the park at twelve-thirty."

"Well, we'd better be careful," Amber said. "The police patrol the park for curfew violators. We'll leave the truck on a side street and walk to the rock."

"Good idea," said Jinx.

Amber drove to the Garcia home. Again she

flashed the headlights three times.

Elena appeared at her bedroom window and waved.

The girls watched as Elena removed the window screen and started to climb out head first. Suddenly she started flailing her arms and bobbing her head up and down.

"What's she doing?" Jinx gasped. "She's going to fall!"

"No, she's not," said Amber. "She's stuck!"

Amber and Jinx rushed from the truck. Half-worried, half-laughing, they positioned themselves under Elena.

"Shhh!" Elena pleaded. "You'll wake my mom!"

"Give us your hands," Amber suggested, "and we'll pull you out."

"Maybe you should cut down on the Rocky Road ice cream," kidded Jinx.

"That's not funny," Elena moaned. She extended her right hand to Amber, and Jinx took her left. The girls tugged gently until Elena popped out like a balloon filled with sand.

"Come on," Amber hissed, "let's get out of here."

The next stop was Kayla's house. Luckily

she was waiting on the porch. "This is so cool," she said, joining Elena in the back of the pick-up, behind the cab.

"It's cool if we don't get caught," Elena murmured.

"Speaking of which, I barely made it," Kayla admitted. "My dad never actually went to bed. He fell asleep in front of the TV. I found him snoring there with the remote still in his hand. I just hope he doesn't wake up and decide to check on me."

"Yeah, I left some pillows bunched up under my covers," Elena said. "But my mom always checks on me during the night. So this had better not take too long."

Overhearing the girls' conversation in the back, Jinx turned to Amber. "If my parents find out, I'll be grounded for the rest of my life."

"And that would mean you couldn't go out with Doug!" teased Amber.

"Will you stop going on about Doug and me?" pleaded Jinx.

"It's too much fun torturing you," Amber said with a devilish grin.

She parked the truck a block from the entrance to the park. The girls walked quickly, making sure no police cars were round. Once in the park they followed the path illuminated by street lights towards the large boulder where they were to meet Lori.

Looking ahead, though, Amber saw no sign of her. "Do you think her parents caught her sneaking out?"

"It would be just like Lori to get caught," said Jinx.

"She'll be here," Kayla assured the others. "She hates being left out of anything."

But, as the minutes crept by, the girls became increasingly worried.

"What if the cops picked Lori up for violating curfew?" said Elena.

"Maybe she fell asleep and never left," whispered Amber.

"Or what if something horrible happened on the way over?" suggested Jinx.

"Will you all stop it?" Kayla said. "That gives me the creeps."

Finally they saw Lori running towards them.

"Sorry," she huffed, out of breath. "Tonight of all nights, my parents decided to stay up late and go over household expenses. I thought they'd never stop fighting and go to bed."

"The important thing is we're all here," Amber said. "OK, I'll go first. I'm not quite sure what happened last night. But I think we should keep quiet about it until we figure it out."

"You mean we all may have imagined it?" Lori asked. "Like some mass hysteria?"

Amber shook her head. "No. I talked to my parents about telekinesis. They did say that it could happen, given the right concentration of mental energy. It's just...well, I'm not sure what it is we've tapped into."

"At dinner, I tried for ages to bend a fork," Kayla said.

"And did it work?" asked Jinx.

Kayla shook her head. "My dad kept looking at me like I'd gone off the deep end."

"I tried to turn off the TV from the couch," Lori added. "Not using the remote, just using my thoughts. And I couldn't get it to work, either."

Jinx and Elena reported similar failed results.

"Maybe it only works when the five of us are together," suggested Amber. "You know the old saying that two heads are better than one. Well, maybe five heads are best of all!"

"I think we imagined the whole thing," said a sceptical Jinx.

Amber looked round. "Let's raise the boulder."

Jinx's eyebrows shot up. "The boulder? It must weigh five tons!"

"We lifted a table not knowing what we were doing," said Kayla. "This boulder should be a piece of cake."

"That's the spirit!" encouraged Amber.

The girls formed a circle in front of the rock and held hands.

"Jinx, you have to really be with us," warned Amber, "or it won't work."

"I'm with you," Jinx assured the others. "I'm just a little freaked."

"Well, it is pretty scary," admitted Elena. "But it's also pretty awesome to think we have such power."

Kayla nodded solemnly. "The power of the girlfriends."

"All right, everybody," Amber ordered. "Concentrate."

The girls shut their eyes.

"In your mind, see the boulder start to vibrate, ever so slowly," Amber said in a hushed voice. "Create the tiniest air space between the bottom of the boulder and the ground. Now focus, really focus."

The girls tightened their grip on each other's hands.

In her own mind, Amber thought of nothing except lifting that enormous slab of granite. She pretended it was not solid rock, but made of cotton. "It's only a big round ball of fluffy light cotton wool."

Opening her eyes, Amber watched the boulder start to lift ever so slowly off the ground.

"We're doing it," she told the other girls.

They opened their eyes and looked at the boulder.

Jinx's lower jaw dropped. "Oh my god," she mumbled.

"Yes!" cried Kayla.

"This is so great!" chimed Lori.

"Don't stop," said Amber. "Let's see if we can raise it above our heads. It's light as a feather."

"It's light as a feather," the girls chanted over and over. "Light as a feather."

The group continued to concentrate. And the boulder continued to inch its way skywards.

"Good!" Amber said, looking at the gigantic rock hovering above them. "Now let's gently lower it back down."

With smiles on their faces, the girls watched

as the boulder descended as if it really was light as a feather. When it gently nestled back on to the ground, the girls hugged one another.

"See?" Amber whispered excitedly. "It only works when we're together."

"All I can say is – wow!" Kayla put her hand to her head and spun in a circle. "Wow."

"We can do anything!" declared Lori proudly. "We have the power."

"We ought to use our new power to make sure we win the All-Conference Rodeo," Elena announced.

Amber rolled her eyes. "Oh, Elena, is the Pep Club all you can think of?"

"What's wrong with using this power to help the school?" Elena protested.

"Don't think so small," said Lori. "We should use this power to help the whole world!"

"And make ourselves rich," added Elena.

"Now that's spoken like the true Taurus material girl," Amber kidded her.

"What we need is a name," Kayla said excitedly. "We need to call ourselves something snappy."

"What about the Spoon Benders?" Elena said as a joke. "No. That sounds like a catering firm."

"How about the Table Lifters?" offered Jinx.

"Table Lifters?" Kayla put both hands on her hips. "Girl, that sounds like a furniture moving company!"

"How about the Morphettes?" suggested Lori.

The other girls rolled their eyes.

"Or the Mindbenders?" suggested Amber.

"Mindbenders," repeated Kayla, trying it out. "That's getting closer, but it's still not quite there." She thought for a few moments, then grinned. "I've got it. Let's call ourselves the Mental Cases!"

"Nice try," Amber said with a smirk. She ran through some other possibilities in her head. "What about an acronym? You know, like the Los Alamos Sisters and Sorcerers Outrageous."

"That's a mouthful," observed Kayla.

"Exactly. We'll go by the initials," Amber replied. "L-A-S-S-O. LASSO. We'll be the secret organization known only as LASSO."

Jinx nodded. "It has a nice Southwestern ring."

"It also keeps what we're doing a total secret," Lori added. "You know. People will think we're cowgirls."

"Cowgirls, out riding the range, lifting

horses and bending barrels," Kayla joked.

Elena checked her watch. "I don't want to be a party pooper, but I'd better get home before Mom does bed check."

"Me, too," added Lori. "I don't want to get busted."

"All right," said Amber. "But before we leave, everyone must swear to keep LASSO a secret."

They each held up a hand and repeated after Amber, "Not a word to any outsider! Our lips are sealed."

Walking back to the truck, Lori pointed to the row of houses across from the park. "That's where my ex-best friend lives," she said bitterly. "Kristal Taylor. That's her bedroom up on the first floor."

All the girls stopped and stared at Kristal's house.

"It wasn't all Kristal's fault that Brad left you," Kayla said, putting an arm round Lori. "He had something to do with it too, you know."

"I know," Lori said, her eyes wet with tears. "But, believe me, she made it very, very easy for him. One day I hope she gets what she deserves for betraying our friendship."

Amber stared at Kristal's upstairs bedroom window, thinking about Christopher and his new girlfriend Emily.

"Maybe we should levitate Kristal out of bed," suggested Elena.

"Let's do it!" said Lori, her eyes flashing with excitement. "That would really frighten her."

Together the girls stared at Kristal's window. At first, nothing seemed to happen.

Then, without warning, all of the upstairs windows blew out of the house! Glass, pieces of wood, and wire-mesh screen flew in every direction.

The girls screamed and took off running down the sidewalk. They could hear shouts of alarm from inside the house. Lights came on all over the neighbourhood.

"What happened?" someone shouted.

"I'm calling 911!" a neighbour yelled from his front door.

"Something blew up at the Taylors!" another voice cried.

"Did a jet crash?" a little boy wailed. "I'm scared."

Reaching the end of the block, Amber shouted to the others, "Follow me!"

She led them across the street and down an alley, just as a fire truck, an ambulance, and several police cars sped towards Kristal's house.

The girls ducked behind a garage to catch their breaths.

"Did we do that?" asked a horrified Elena.

"I was just trying to lift Kristal out of bed," said Lori.

"Me, too," added Jinx.

They could hear the commotion as Kristal's family ran screaming from the house, and police and firemen ran in.

"Nobody move," Amber ordered. "We stay right here until things quieten down."

Kayla was shocked. "How could that happen?"

"We caused it," whimpered a guilt-ridden Lori. "We must've concentrated too hard – or thought the wrong thoughts – or something!"

"And here I was worried about sneaking out," added a stricken Elena.

"Everybody, put your hands on mine," ordered Amber. She extended her right hand.

"What for?" asked Jinx.

"Just do it!" Amber said.

The girls placed their hands in a stack on top

of Amber's. "This is the end of LASSO," Amber said, her voice trembling. "Let us take a solemn vow that we will never, ever, *ever* use our power again."

"The end of LASSO," the other girls agreed. "Never, ever again."

CHAPTER SIX

Power is building up for you in local situations, everyday matters and studies. But an aspect between Mars and Uranus transiting in the sky will act like a burr under your saddle. Ignore it and press ahead.

On Monday, the girls gathered in the quad during lunch.

"Lori...your hair!" Amber said, gaping at her friend.

Lori had not only washed her hair but had used a curling iron to give it a bouncy wave. "Do you like it?" she asked. She was even wearing a little make-up, something she never did.

"Major improvement," Kayla said. "What gives?"

"I guess I'm feeling better about things," Lori explained. Then she ducked her head lower and whispered, "I have to confess – it's great having a little power."

"Speaking of which – did you see Kristal?" asked Elena with a mixture of horror and glee.

Jinx nodded. "Bandages all up and down her arms," she said, trying not to smile. "And one right across her face."

"She looks like a Mummy," joked Kayla.

Elena, Lori, and Jinx began to laugh.

"This isn't funny," Amber said sternly. "We could get kicked out of school – or worse! We could all be charged with malicious mischief, or something."

"I overheard Kristal telling Marnee that her family is so freaked out that they've moved into a motel," Jinx reported. "They're staying there until they figure out what caused the explosion."

"Well, none of this leaves our group," said Amber. She took a moment to stare each girl in the eye until they all nodded. "We had our fun. Remember, we swore never, ever again."

"At least, if something bad had to happen, I'm glad it happened to snotty Kristal Taylor," sneered Jinx.

"Yeah," Lori said. "I wonder how Brad will like his new girlfriend looking like an escapee from *General Hospital*."

"I said, enough!" snapped Amber, barely controlling her temper.

"Hey, girlfriend," Kayla advised. "Chill!"

"I'm sorry," Amber said. "I didn't sleep very well."

The girls deliberately changed the subject. They covered the auditions on Wednesday for *Sweeney Todd*. The possibility of Doug asking Jinx to the senior prom. They even placed bets on whether or not Elena would sell her last rodeo ticket before the end of lunch period that day.

The girls had all but put the explosion episode behind them when a sophomore girl, Colleen Simmons, walked over to the table.

"Can I ask you guys a favour?" she said in a voice barely above a whisper.

The group looked at each other, surprised. They hardly knew Colleen.

"What kind of favour?" Kayla finally asked.

"My dog Elsie got out of our back yard and was picked up by animal control," Colleen explained. "Elsie's in the pound. If I don't get her out, they'll destroy her. The problem is, my dad won't give me the money to pay the fine and I don't have any money."

"So you want to borrow some money?" asked Amber.

"Sorry." Jinx held up both hands. "I spent my last five dollars on Elena's rodeo ticket."

"No, no, you don't understand," Colleen said, nervously pushing her frizzy brown hair out of her eyes. "I thought you – all of you – might be able to help me. The pound closes at five, so no one's there after that."

"You want us to break into the pound?" asked Lori.

"No, nothing like that," Colleen insisted. "You see, Elsie and the other dogs are kept in a fenced-in area outside the building. But there's no roof on the fence. If I could just get Elsie lifted over the fence, she'd be free."

"Lifted?" Amber repeated, her eyes widening.

"Yeah, like you did to that boulder in the park," Colleen said, as if that were common knowledge.

Amber shot the other girls a "who told?" look.

They all avoided looking at her and stared at the table top or their hands in their laps.

Amber turned back to Colleen. "We'll think about it and get back to you. You'd better go now. And if you breathe a word of this to anyone – we definitely won't help rescue your dog."

"I swear I won't tell anyone," Colleen said, backing away from the group. "Thank you. Thank you."

Amber glared at the group. "Do you want to get us kicked out of school? Or arrested?" She started with Jinx. "Did you tell anyone?"

Jinx slumped guiltily on her bench. "I accidentally woke my little sister when I snuck home last night. She threatened to tell our parents if I didn't tell her what I'd been doing."

"And your sister's in Colleen's class," Amber concluded with a sigh.

"True," said Jinx. "But I don't think she'd tell – she's usually really good with secrets."

"Elena, how about you?" asked Amber.

Elena blushed. "I told my cousin. I know I swore not to, but it was too good a story not to share."

"Great," Amber said, shaking her head. "Kayla?"

"I mentioned it to Colleen's older sister on the bus this morning," Kayla confessed, without lifting her eyes.

"Lori?" Amber continued round the circle.

"I, ah, mentioned to Brad that I heard what happened to Kristal," Lori admitted. "But I swear I didn't tell him we had anything to do with it."

"This is great," Amber muttered. "Just great! Each of you needs to find whoever you told and swear them to absolute secrecy."

The girls, all looking very sheepish, agreed.

"Amber," Jinx said quietly, "can't we help Colleen? Her mom died last year and that mangy dog Elsie is all she has."

"Yeah, Amber," Lori chimed in. "Can't LASSO get together one last time?"

Elena and Kayla nodded their approval.

Amber hesitated. This power they'd tapped into had so far been used only for destruction. It would be nice to do a good deed.

"OK," Amber said. "Let's meet at the pound at five-thirty. But not a word of this to anyone!"

The girls crossed their hearts and pretended to button their lips, swearing to keep it secret.

After lunch Amber walked down the hall towards her locker. Normally only her friends noticed her. But today it seemed nearly every student stopped what they were doing as she walked by.

Christopher and his buddies huddled together round his locker. He whispered something to the group. After hearing it, they stared at Amber, shaking their heads.

Further down the hall, Marnee Moziman whispered something to Doug Farber and to Elena's boyfriend, Joe. The three went completely silent as Amber passed.

Even cocky Troy Evans and his cowboy pals stopped talking when Amber approached.

Weird. Does everyone know about LASSO? Amber shook her head and adjusted her glasses. *You're just being paranoid.* Besides, if they did know, they'd say something, a joke, a jab, something.

After school, Amber told her parents that she and her friends had to work on their science project together.

"What about dinner?" her mother asked.

"I'll pick up a burrito somewhere," Amber said. "Don't worry."

"And what time will you be back?" her father asked.

"I don't know. Eight or nine o'clock," Amber said. "I promised Kayla I'd listen to her audition piece."

Her parents smiled and nodded. Obviously they had no clue what was going on.

"Just feed Patsy — and your other pets — before you leave," Amber's mother reminded.

Amber and Kayla were first to arrive at the

pound. They waited outside in Amber's pick-up until the last employee locked the door on his way out.

"Come on," Kayla said. "It's safe now."

The girls walked round the building to the back, where dozens of dogs were confined behind a tall chain-link fence.

"I'm not sure this is such a good idea," said Amber.

"If the five of us can lift a five-ton boulder," said Kayla, "some fuzzy-faced mutt will be easy."

"It's not that," Amber said. "I'm worried that maybe we've unleashed something that we can't control."

"Of course we can control it," Kayla said. "Do you see rocks floating in the sky? Windows exploding every time we pass by? Girl, get a grip!"

"OK, up till now we've controlled the power," Amber conceded. "But one day it may control us."

"Amber, we're not blowing up the world here," Kayla said. "We're rescuing Colleen's little dog. Hardly earth-shattering."

"True," Amber said with a nod.

The other three girls — and Colleen — arrived.

"Sorry we're late," said Lori. "My mom insisted I eat a large snack before I left. I had to gag down celery sticks stuffed with cream cheese and raisins."

"There she is!" Colleen shouted. She bent down by the fence as a wire-haired terrier raced up. The dog whined and poked its nose through the fence for Colleen to pet. "Oh, Elsie! Don't worry, girl. I'll get you out."

"Can we get started soon?" Kayla asked. "I need to go home and work on my audition for *Sweeney Todd*."

"Colleen, you have to wait round the corner," Amber instructed.

The girl looked disappointed. "Can't I watch?" Colleen asked.

"No." The idea of tapping into some vast, unknown power was making Amber feel increasingly on edge. "Do you want Elsie back or not?"

"Just don't hurt her, OK?" Colleen pleaded, backing round the corner.

"Let's get this over with," Amber snapped. She put out her hands for Jinx and Kayla to hold.

Forming a circle, the girls closed their eyes for a few moments, focusing their minds on the task of rescuing the dog.

"In your mind, see Elsie as light as a feather," Amber said in even tones. "See Elsie slowly rise. Slowly, so she doesn't get frightened." She opened her eyes and continued to chant. "Up. Up. She's light as a feather."

"Light as a feather," the group repeated.

"That's it," Amber whispered.

The other girls opened their eyes to the strange sight of a dog floating in the air. Elsie, looking round, not knowing what to make of it, stuck her legs stiffly out beneath her as she rose above the fence and slowly descended to the other side. Free.

"That's it," Amber cried as the dog touched the ground. "We did it."

"Colleen!" Kayla shouted. "Come and get your little mutt!"

An ecstatic Colleen ran round the corner. Upon seeing Elsie, she began to cry. Scooping the dog up in her arms, she said, "Oh, thank you. You don't know what she means to me. Thank you all so much!"

Even Amber had to admit that this time LASSO had done a good deed.

"Colleen, would you mind waiting round the front?" asked Amber.

The girl happily complied. After she was gone, Amber told the others, "OK, we saved a dog. We did our good deed for the day. But now it's time to quit."

"Quit?" repeated Kayla, obviously disappointed.

"Let's quit before someone gets hurt," Amber insisted. "The end of LASSO. The end of this crazy idea that we can control something that we don't understand. It's time to put the genie back in the bottle for good."

The other girls reluctantly agreed. All except Kayla. She was shaking her head, "No."

"Do you have something to say?" Amber asked her.

"Hey, I agree with everything you said," Kayla began. "This telekinesis thing could get out of hand, no question."

"Well?" Amber said.

"It just bugs me that we helped outsiders before helping each other."

"She's right," Lori said. "We should each get one wish granted before we stop for good!"

Amber looked round the circle. Each of the others was nodding vigorously, repeating, "One wish."

Amber shoved her glasses up on her nose

and turned to Kayla. "All right, Kayla, what's this about?"

Kayla took a deep breath and let it out slowly. "I'll stop," she began. "I really will. But first I've got this little favour to ask..."

CHAPTER SEVEN

Right now, Aquarius has a ruling planet that is industrious and electric in its application. Whatever project you have in mind has Saturn frowning on it. There's a square in the sky that indicates Saturn and Uranus are hurling surprises at each other. Keep out of the way of the fallout.

When the girls arrived at the high school on Wednesday, the auditions for *Sweeney Todd* were already underway in the auditorium. They took seats in the last row, so as not to disrupt what was happening on stage.

The drama teacher, Cynthia Whittle, sat in a row all by herself, taking notes on a clipboard. "Jack Eagle Rock, you're next!" she called out.

Jack, a shy junior with long black hair he kept tied back in a ponytail, entered and stopped in the middle of the stage. "I'm doing a song from Les Miz. I'll be playing the part of

Javert, the villain."

For the next two minutes, Jack sang the dramatic song from the hit show, *Les Miserables*.

"He'll get the part of Sweeney Todd," Kayla whispered. "He's one of the best actors and singers in school."

When Jack finished, he stepped forward and became shy again. Ms Whittle asked him a few questions about his after-school schedule. Finally she said that the callback list — the people she wanted to audition a second time — would be posted at nine the next morning on the bulletin board outside the theatre office.

Ms Whittle looked at her clipboard, then called, "Marnee, you're up!"

The girls watched a very confident Marnee Moziman stroll on to the stage. Marnee was wearing an apron over her dress. She obviously wanted the lead role of Mrs Lovett, the cook. Her long auburn hair was pulled into a bun at the base of her neck and she held a rolling pin in one hand.

"I can't believe her," Jinx whispered. "She comes to the audition practically in costume."

"She has Ms Whittle wrapped round her little finger," Kayla whispered back.

"Especially since Marnee's parents donated five hundred dollars to the theatre programme."

"Here I am," Marnee called from the stage. "Mrs Lovett, at your service." She held the rolling pin across her middle and bowed. She seemed very relaxed.

"Marnee, you don't have to do a song for me," Ms Whittle said. "I'm very familiar with the calibre of your singing."

"Would you like me to bake a pie, luv?" Marnee quipped, in a phony Cockney accent. "Meat pies are me speciality."

"God, she's cocky!" Kayla groaned.

"Very funny," Ms Whittle laughed.

"So do I get the part?" Marnee raised her rolling pin menacingly at Ms Whittle.

"Let's not jump the gun, Marnee," Ms Whittle said. "First, I would like you and Jamie to read a bit from the script. Jamie? Are you there?"

Jamie Thornton, a funny-looking, freckled redhead appeared from the wings.

"I don't mind if Jamie gets a lead part," whispered Kayla. "At least he deserves it. He's *sooo* talented."

He carried with him two copies of the script for *Sweeney Todd*, one of which he handed to

Marnee.

"Top of page thirty," Ms Whittle said. "And, Jamie, you start with Todd's speech. Find it?"

Turning the scripts to the right page and finding the exact spot, Jamie and Marnee nodded.

"Watch her blow Ms Whittle's socks off." Kayla squeezed her eyes shut and covered her ears. "I can't bear it."

Amber reached out her hands. "Give me your hands. Let's see what we can do."

The girls held hands and stared at the stage. All of them focused their energy at Marnee.

Marnee and Jamie were about to start – when suddenly the script flopped out of Marnee's hand.

She giggled. "Sorry. Guess it just slipped." She bent down to pick it up. With a glance at Jamie, she signalled her readiness to start over.

But again the script seemed to leap from her hands, and slide across the stage.

"Marnee, I think you've clowned round enough," Ms Whittle said. Her voice was tight and clipped, and it was obvious she was getting a bit aggravated by the delay.

"I'm so sorry," said a flustered Marnee. "It really was an accident." When she picked the script up she turned it over, to see if something was attached to it.

"Marnee, what's the problem now?" Ms Whittle said testily.

"Nothing! Nothing!" Marnee snapped back. She was losing her cool.

She returned to Jamie at centre stage. They were about to begin when the script shot out of her hands a third time.

"Want to switch books with me?" asked Jamie, as he hurried to get her script.

"Maybe," Marnee rasped loudly. "I don't know what's going on here."

From the auditorium, Ms Whittle boomed, "All right, you two, what seems to be the problem?"

"I don't know!" Marnee shouted. "This script keeps hopping out of my hands. It's not my fault!"

"Really?" Ms Whittle's voice dripped with sarcasm.

Marnee put her rolling pin on her hip insisting. "I'm *not* doing it."

"Maybe you need some time to collect yourself," Ms Whittle suggested. "Why don't you come back in fifteen minutes?"

"I could hold the script," Jamie said, stepping forward, "and Marnee could read from mine."

"Fine," said Ms Whittle with a loud sigh. "Just get on with it."

Marnee stood next to Jamie. He recited the first line perfectly. But when it was time to respond, Marnee turned to Ms Whittle and blubbered, "The page keeps moving. I can't read it. The words are jumping round."

Amber and the girls had already let go of each other's hands. "Now she really is losing it," Amber whispered.

Jinx and Lori had to cover their mouths to keep from laughing.

"Just get through one page," Ms Whittle ordered. She was totally exasperated. "Really, Marnee, this is really trying my patience..."

Marnee was so angry that she made no sense of anything on the page. She read Jamie's part by mistake. She read the stage directions, thinking they were her lines. Her audition was a fiasco.

"Thank you, Marnee and Jamie," Ms Whittle said, crossing Marnee's name off her list. "Hugh Wheldon is next and Kayla Johnson is on deck."

"Thanks, you guys," Kayla whispered to the other girls as she gathered her sheet music. "I almost feel bad for her."

"Don't worry about Marnee," whispered Amber. "She's history. Just get up there and win!"

The next day after school, Amber and Jinx drove to the ranch to go riding.

"I can't get over the look on Marnee's face when that script went flying," Amber said, shaking her head.

"Hey, she had it coming for all the snotty things she's done in the past," Jinx reminded her. "And Kayla *is* more talented. Even if it took something like yesterday for Ms 'Wit-less' to notice."

"Kayla told me that Marnee didn't make the callback list," Amber added. "So Marnee's out of the show completely."

"Yes!" Jinx pumped her fist in the air. "There *is* justice!"

Amber beeped the horn in agreement.

"I know it's kind of evil what we did," Jinx said with a happy sigh. "But it sure was fun."

"Well, that's the end of LASSO," Amber reminded her. "Kayla has her wish now."

"Elena thinks that since Kayla got a favour, she should, too," Jinx informed Amber.

"What does Elena want?"

"For us to use our power to help Los Alamos West take the rodeo title," Jinx said.

"Out of the question," Amber said, flicking on her signal to turn into the Double R Stables.

"Why does Kayla get to use the power and the rest of us don't?" Jinx asked, slumping down in the seat. She was pouting like a five-year-old.

"Just because," Amber said, easing the truck into a parking slot and putting an end to the discussion.

The girls hopped out of the truck and headed for the barn.

"Amber," Jinx tugged on the sleeve of her jean jacket. "Look who's here."

Christopher was waiting outside the stables.

"It looks like he's alone," Amber whispered out of the corner of her mouth.

"Yeah, I don't see Emily, the living Barbie doll," Jinx whispered back. "I bet he's here to beg you to take him back."

"Fat chance," muttered Amber.

"You watch," Jinx predicted. "He'll be on his hands and knees, pleading for forgiveness."

"Hey, Jinx," Christopher said, moving to meet them. "I need a few minutes alone with

Amber. Would you mind?"

"Oh, of course not," Jinx said, winking at Amber. "You know where to find me."

Jinx was barely out of hearing distance when Christopher faced Amber and said stiffly, "We need to talk."

Amber was stunned at the chill in his tone. "We do? I don't think so." Amber's hurt was coming back. She could feel the dark knot start to form deep inside her head.

"Amber, this is serious," Christopher said.

"Look, Christopher, I'm here to ride," Amber said, making a wide arc to get round him. "If you need to talk to me, you'll have to do it while I saddle Riley."

"Fine." Christopher followed her inside the stables, where she took her horse from his stall.

"So what's so important?" she asked, taking Riley's bridle from the wall and slipping it over the horse's head. "So important you have to talk to me right now?"

"Amber, what's this weird rumour I've been hearing about a group called LASSO?" he asked.

"Group?" she repeated innocently. "Sounds like a country and western band."

"Don't play dumb, Amber," he said, taking

her arm.

She stared at his hand, waiting for him to release her. Then she said coldly, "I don't know anything about a group named LASSO."

"That's strange," Christopher replied. "Because the rumour is you're the head of it."

Amber looped Riley's reins round the post in the corral. Then she went back into the tack room, grabbed her horse's blanket and saddle, and returned outside. "Where did you hear this rumour?" she asked.

"All the kids at school are talking about it," he said. "They say you and your pals are messing round with witchcraft."

She stared at him. "Witchcraft?" A slow smile crossed her lips. "In that case – shazam! You're a nice guy!"

Christopher frowned at her and sighed.

"Oh, guess it's not working," she said sarcastically.

Christopher was not going to budge. He looked her straight in the eye and said, "The story I heard is that things got out of control at your slumber party last Friday."

"Oh, puh-leeze!" Amber made sure the blanket was flat and even across Riley's back before swinging the saddle into place. "We read our horoscopes and played with a Ouija board. That's all."

She reached under Riley's belly to grab the girth and buckled it high on the other side so the saddle wouldn't slip.

"I heard some other things which might interest you," he continued.

"Like?"

Christopher stepped between Amber and the horse, forcing her to listen. "Like stories about a dog being lifted in the air. And Marnee Moziman insisting that something kept yanking her script out of her hand at the auditions."

"Marnee Moziman?" scoffed Amber. "She's just trying to make excuses for blowing her big chance to be in the play."

"OK, then what about Kristal Taylor's windows?" He was staring straight into her eyes.

"What about them?" she said, holding his gaze.

He cocked his head. "You didn't have anything to do with that? Kristal heard you did."

"Well, good for Kristal." Amber could feel the knot forming inside her. It was becoming harder and harder to keep that knot from exploding.

Trying to distract herself, Amber grabbed a currycomb that had been left lying on the fence and tried to clear some tangles from Riley's tail.

"Amber, why won't you talk to me?" Christopher asked, moving round to her side.

"I am talking," she insisted. But her mind was going a million miles a second. *Who's the giant blabbermouth? Someone is trying to get us all in trouble.*

She was so angry that the currycomb flew out of her hands. It struck the fence post and ricochetted back at high speed. Chris had to leap backwards to avoid the comb's path.

"What are you doing!" he cried. "Are you trying to kill me?"

"It wasn't me," she said, forcing herself to stay calm. "Must have been the pony's tail."

"A horse couldn't have done that," Christopher insisted. Amber could hear the fear in his voice. "This is just the kind of thing I'm talking about."

Amber was sick of being given the third degree. She threw her hands in the air. "What does any of this have to do with you, anyway?" she rasped. "We broke up. Remember?"

Christopher ran both hands through his hair.

"Amber, I'm worried that you might be into something you can't handle."

Amber couldn't believe her ears. She started to walk away from him, then changed her mind and turned to confront him. "Two weeks ago, out of the blue, you tell me to get out of your life. Now you're worried about me and won't leave me alone. I don't get it."

"Maybe I'm confused," he said sincerely. "Amber, I can understand if you don't believe me – given what I did. But the reason I broke it off is because...well, you scare me sometimes."

She choked out a laugh. "I scare you. That's a good one."

"Don't believe it then," he said quietly.

Amber turned her back and squeezed her eyes shut. *Maybe he is being sincere. Maybe he's changed his mind and wants me back.*

"Chris, since we're finally talking – really talking," she said in a much softer voice, "there are a few things you should know." Amber spun back to face him. "It all started when –" She stopped, detecting a real wariness in his eyes. "Never mind."

Amber moved to Riley and was about to put her left foot into the stirrup and swing herself up when the stirrup jumped out of her reach. *That's weird. I didn't do that. Riley must have moved.*

"Chris," she said, looking over her shoulder, "would you give me a hand?"

"A hand?"

"Hold the stirrup," Amber asked. "Just for a second."

But he remained frozen.

"Chris..." She put her hand out to touch him – and he flinched, stepping away.

"Amber, don't."

"Chris, are you afraid of me?" The thought almost made her laugh. But his cold, distant expression chilled even the faintest smile.

"Should I be?" he asked in a hollow voice.

CHAPTER EIGHT

If you want a new start in life, this is your week to do it. The favourable aspects are as orderly as geese flying south. The Moon in Leo widens your horizons and softens all edges. But don't let down your guard completely. A snake could be lurking in the grass.

"This is so bo-ring!" Amber whispered to Jinx. The girls were seated together at an all-school assembly the following week. Kayla sat on the other side of Jinx. Her eyes were closed and she looked as if she was taking a nap. Lori was playing tic-tac-toe in her notebook with Elena.

Mrs Cantwell, their Ancient History teacher, was up on stage droning into a microphone. "Graduation is only a few short months away for you seniors. Many of you are already old enough to vote and to serve in our armed forces.

Now, one day you young people will inherit the responsibility of running this country," she said in the flattest monotone possible. "This responsibility is not something to be taken lightly..."

"I hate this," Amber whispered. Her head was pounding. She massaged her temples and the back of her neck, but it didn't bring the slightest relief.

"We should blow Cantwell off the stage," suggested Lori. "That would be exciting."

Elena nodded. "We should do something, for sure."

Jinx's face lit up with an impish smile. "I've got it," she whispered to the others. "Let's have some fun with the PA system."

Amber didn't think this was such a great plan, but she agreed that Mrs Cantwell had to be stopped before she bored the entire school to death.

So the girls held hands, and each focused on Mrs Cantwell.

"To prepare yourselves to become contributing members of society, you must realize the importance of a thorough education, which is—" Suddenly Mrs Cantwell could no longer be heard over the auditorium speakers.

Not that she noticed at first. She continued to speak into the now dead microphone.

"It's working!" Lori exclaimed.

Students began to giggle at the teacher's predicament.

Just as she realized something was going on, the speakers came back on. "As I was saying," she continued, "education is something you should take lightly only at your own peril—"

Her words became silent again.

The auditorium began to ripple with laughter.

Mrs Cantwell stopped. She examined the microphone, although it was clear she knew nothing about it. Still, she fiddled with the cord and pushed the on-off button a few times. She was tapping the top when suddenly the sound blasted through the auditorium, like a string of bombs going off.

The noise caused Mrs Cantwell to spring back and put a hand to her chest – to the delight of the students.

Amber and her friends covered their mouths, trying desperately not to call attention to themselves.

But one by one, students began to turn in their seats to look at the girls.

"They know we did it," Jinx told the others.

"Don't say a word," Amber warned. "I mean it."

Totally flustered, Mrs Cantwell had to leave the stage. For this she received a standing ovation.

With the assembly broken up, the students headed out of the auditorium. Many, including Amber and her friends, took advantage of the unexpected recess to mingle in the hall.

"Did you see everyone turn round and look at us?" she asked. "Who is doing the talking?"

"It's not me," swore Jinx. "I can keep a secret."

"Well, I'm not telling a soul," Kayla insisted. "I'm keeping my mouth shut because I don't want to lose the part I got in *Sweeney Todd*."

"You got the part?" said Lori.

Kayla nodded. "Ms Whittle asked me not to say anything until she posted the cast list this afternoon," she explained. "So don't spread the word – especially to Marnee. But I get to play Mrs Lovett."

"That's so great!" Elena said, giving Kayla a big hug.

"Elena, did you spill the beans about LASSO?" asked Amber.

"No way!" Elena replied. "My mother is looking for any reason to ground me. Well, I'm not giving her any cause. Especially with the rodeo coming up."

"Lori?" Amber barked.

"Why don't you lay off?" Jinx said, placing her hand on Amber's shoulder. "We're your friends. Remember? You're grilling us like we murdered someone."

"One of you has to be leaking this," Amber insisted.

"How do we know that *you're* not the guilty party?" said Jinx.

"Why would I ruin my reputation?" responded Amber.

"Well, why would any of us?" asked Kayla.

"I haven't told," Lori said. "But I'm kind of glad it's got out."

"Why?" asked Amber.

"Because for the first time since I hit high school I feel like I'm somebody," Lori explained. "That I'm worth something. Look at the other kids." She gestured to the students passing by. "See the looks of awe on their faces?"

"Lori's right," agreed Elena. "I'm not saying we shouldn't be careful – we should. But it's great to get some respect."

"And even better to have self-appointed stars like Kristal and Marnee scared of us," added Kayla.

Amber felt very confused. In all her years in school she'd been a well-liked but largely invisible presence. Her friends were right. Now they were getting a great deal of attention. But was it the right kind of attention?

Johnny Diamond, a neighbour of Kayla's, rushed up to the girls. "I need you guys to help me," he said in a panic.

"What's up?" Kayla asked.

"I took my dad's car to school today without asking," Johnny explained.

"Are you crazy?" Kayla cut in. She turned to the other girls and said, "Johnny's dad loves that car more than he does Johnny."

Johnny nodded. "Sad, but true."

"You didn't wreck it, did you?" asked Lori.

"No. I locked the keys in the car," he said. "Help me get them out so my old man doesn't come home from work, find the car gone, and murder me."

The girls looked at Amber, waiting for her decision.

She let out a reluctant sigh. "All right, I

suppose we'll have to help."

The girls and Johnny headed for the parking lot. He looked very relieved.

"See?" Elena said to Amber. "Isn't it great that we can do things to help others?"

Amber shrugged her shoulders. "I suppose."

"It *is* great," insisted Jinx. "I just wish I could do things alone. I still can't make even a dent in a spoon when I try it at home."

"Neither can I," added Lori. "It only works when we're all together."

"Other than that first time with the spoon," Amber said, "it's only worked when I'm with you guys."

Arriving at the car, the girls quickly held hands.

"Turn your back, Johnny," ordered Amber.

"Can't I watch how you do it?" he asked.

Amber narrowed her eyes at him. "Do you want the keys or not?"

Johnny quickly turned round and covered his eyes.

Amber said to the other girls, "The easiest thing is to lift up the door lock knob. With the door unlocked, he can easily get the keys."

Doing it before anyone else took notice, the girls focused on the door lock until the knob shot upwards as if yanked by an invisible force.

"OK, Johnny," said Kayla. "We saved your sorry butt!"

"Thanks a lot," he said, giving her a hug and half bowing towards the rest of the girls. "I swear I won't tell."

As the girls headed back to the main building they discovered Rachel Martinez, a senior from Amber's home room, in tears. Rachel was hiding between two cars, apparently so no one would see how upset she was, and holding her face in her hands.

"Rachel, what's the matter?" asked Amber, rushing over to her.

"It's Troy," Rachel said between sobs. "He's such a jerk!"

"What did he do now?" Elena asked.

Rachel and Troy Evans had a tempestuous relationship. More than once an argument had broken out between them in the school halls.

Rachel slowly lowered a hand which had been covering the side of her face, exposing a bruise below her left eye.

"The jerk did that?" Kayla fumed.

Rachel nodded. "He said he was dumping me. When I asked him why, he said I was too boring to bother with, and did this."

Jinx's nostrils were flaring. "Where is he now?"

Rachel pointed to another part of the parking lot where Troy was sitting on the bonnet of a car with a few of his cowboy buddies from the rodeo squad. He was laughing and having a grand time.

"I *hate* boys!" snarled Amber as she stared at the group.

"Me too," added Lori. "They think they're so cool and powerful."

"Troy needs to learn that he should never ever hit a girl," Amber whispered, continuing to glare at the boys. Her head was throbbing. She felt herself slowly slipping into a deep and dangerous whirlpool of her own creation.

The girls eyed one another. They had no intention of letting this opportunity pass them by.

"Come on." Amber extended her hands.

The girls joined their circle and focused their wrath in Troy's direction.

Suddenly Troy stopped laughing. He quickly clutched his throat, as if something was choking him. His eyes widened. Without warning, as if pulled by an invisible cord, he spun off the bonnet of the car and slammed into

119

a pick-up truck parked nearby.

It was obvious that he didn't know what had hit him. He struggled to his feet, holding his ribs.

By now his rodeo buddies had stopped laughing. One of them pointed in the girls' direction. Troy looked up and paled.

"He's afraid of us!" Jinx cried.

"All right!" added Lori.

"Take that, sucker!" shouted Kayla.

"He deserved it," observed Elena.

Rachel had stopped crying and her eyes were two wide circles. "Um, thanks, you guys," she stammered. "But I didn't mean for you to—"

"He deserved it," Jinx cut her off.

Amber said nothing. The dark knot was so painful it caused her to lower her head.

"Girl, are you OK?" asked Kayla.

"I don't know how great this is at all," Amber managed to say. Her temples were pounding. "It's starting to make me feel a little crazy."

"Maybe you're just hungry," Kayla suggested. "A hit or two of chocolate will fix you right up!"

But it wasn't hunger. Amber needed to talk to someone, someone she could trust – and soon.

CHAPTER NINE

*T*hat night Amber waited for her dad to go to bed before knocking on her mother's study door. As was her habit, Harriet was working late at her computer. She said she enjoyed the privacy and quiet – and the close proximity of the well-stocked refrigerator.

"Mom," Amber asked. "Do you have a few minutes?"

Harriet turned round from the computer that occupied the centre of her desk which was crowded with reports, books, and technical manuals.

"Of course, dear," she said. "Just let me save my work on the hard drive." She turned back and typed in some commands. "Now I'll back it up on a floppy."

Mom, always teaching by example, Amber thought. She couldn't believe how quickly her mother's fingers worked the keyboard. But both of her parents were geniuses. She herself was smart, more clever than brilliant. *And sometimes, like now, not even that clever.*

Harriet left the computer on. No doubt she would return to work after their chat. But she turned down the classical music she had been listening to, and moved to the sofa covered with a Navajo blanket.

"We don't get to talk much nowadays," she said, patting the cushion next to her. "Between my schedule and your schedule and Stefan's schedule, it's hard to connect. What's on your mind?"

Amber sat down next to Harriet. She felt close to her mother. They'd almost always got on together. But she felt nervous and didn't know where to start.

Perhaps sensing this, Harriet said, "Amber, you've seemed very distracted these past few weeks. You're rarely home. And I can't remember the last time I saw you playing with Patsy in the back yard."

Amber nodded. She appreciated that her mother was trying to start the conversation. "Mom, this may sound like a weird question," she said, "but was I an unusual child?"

Harriet smiled and took a few moments to

answer. "Yes," she finally said. "And you are an unusual teenager."

"Mom!" protested Amber.

"I mean it as a compliment," Harriet said, taking Amber by the hand. "You're growing up so quickly." Her voice was full of emotion. "You're a smart and beautiful young woman."

"No, I'm not."

"Yes, you are," Harriet insisted, smoothing Amber's hair away from her forehead. "I don't know if I've ever told you the whole story – but you know I had a great deal of trouble getting pregnant."

Amber nodded. "I know you had a couple of miscarriages before you got pregnant with me."

Harriet nodded sadly at the memory. "I thought I'd never be able to carry a baby. Then, long after Stefan and I had given up hope, I became pregnant – with you."

"Didn't you and Dad think the problem might be side effects from all of the atomic radiation round here?"

"To this day," her mother said quietly, "I don't think we scientists know fully how radiation affects the human body. Yes, we considered that somehow the radiation might have contributed to the failed pregnancies.

123

Between the atomic tests and the many deserted uranium mines in the area, there are unusually high radioactive levels recorded here. But when I did become pregnant for the last time – and it was evident that I would carry you to term – I was so happy, I forgot all about it."

Amber felt embarrassed seeing her mother display so much emotion.

"Not that it was an easy pregnancy," Harriet continued. "It wasn't. I worried that something awful might happen and end it too soon. And you were not an easy passenger, believe me."

"What does that mean?" asked Amber.

"You had a mind of your own, from the very beginning," Harriet explained. "If you didn't like what I ate, you'd let me know by kicking and hitting me in the ribs!"

"Oh, come on, Mom! You aren't serious!"

Her mother nodded emphatically. "You loathed broccoli."

"Still do," Amber said, wrinkling her nose.

"And you couldn't stand any tomato sauces," Harriet continued. "You had me eating pasta and butter with just a smidgen of grated cheese on top. And you loved yogurt. You'd punish me if the Mexican food I ate was too spicy for your taste. You—"

"Well, well, what do we have here?" Amber's father asked, entering with a tray of steaming mugs of herbal tea. "A stroll down memory lane?"

"I thought you'd gone to bed," Amber said.

"I did," Stefan said. "But something woke me. Hearing you two chatting, I decided to make some tea. I've always loved the sound of women's voices." He looked at Harriet and Amber. "I'm not interrupting, am I?"

"I was asking Mom about what I was like when I was younger," Amber told him. "Please stay."

He distributed the mugs of tea, then sat down. "Amber, you were a true Aquarian baby."

"Aquarian?" she repeated. "I thought you didn't believe in astrology."

"Oh, the jury is still out," Stefan said. "But I think astrology may help explain some things. For instance, often a baby's eyes will change colour in the first year. But yours never did. You've had the same big grey Aquarian eyes since the day you were born. Beautiful grey eyes – but old and wise beyond their years."

"Stefan's right," Harriet agreed. "You almost

never cried. You just watched and absorbed everything in your field of vision. We sensed you were listening, observing – learning from day one."

"Which is why we weren't at all surprised when you started to talk – and talk in complete sentences – before your first birthday," Stefan added. "Believe it or not, your first words were, 'Mommy, baby not happy'!"

"By the age of two you were already playing piano," remembered Harriet. "You knew the names of various breeds of horses by the time you were three."

"We'd go out for walks," Stefan added, "and you'd recite the names of every flower and tree we passed. By the age of five, you knew more world geography than either Harriet or I."

Harriet nodded and stopped for a sip of tea. "Stranger still, you seemed to know what we were thinking before we said it. You knew when someone was at the door or when the phone was going to ring."

"You started your own projects," Stefan said, "taking things apart to see how they worked, early on." He chuckled at something.

"What?" Amber asked.

"I remember coming home one day and

discovering that you had taken apart our only telephone," he related with a grin. "You said you wanted to find the voices inside."

"You were always very self-sufficient," Harriet said. "Which is a mixed blessing for a parent. I mean, it's quite wonderful when a child can take care of herself. Get herself dressed. Tie her own shoelaces. But it's also nice to do something for the child you love. It was a rare occasion, Amber, when either Stefan or I was able to do something for you." This last part she said almost wistfully.

"Did I have a temper as a kid?" Amber asked, wanting to discuss the dark knot she felt inside her.

Harriet and Stefan glanced at each other. Then Harriet said, "The only time you'd get really, really angry was when we tried to put limits on you. Yes, I'd have to say you had a fierce temper." She chuckled. "It's easy to laugh now, but at the time it wasn't so funny."

"What wasn't?" asked Amber.

"You were three years old, maybe four," Harriet began. "We were all in the family room. It was well past dark. So I told you to quit working on a jigsaw puzzle and get ready for bed. You were furious that I would dare say this."

Harriet exchanged a look with Stefan. For half a second, Amber detected something in their expressions. Fear? Was this memory frightening both her parents?

"Mom...what happened?" Amber said, her voice choking slightly.

"You wouldn't obey me," Harriet said in a quiet tone. "So I asked your father to try. Well, you wouldn't obey him either."

Stefan took up the story. "I had to pick you up and carry you to your room," he said. "You were out of control. Flailing your arms and legs against your bed. Screaming at the top of your lungs."

"I tried to console you," Harriet said. "We both did. But nothing would work. We were worried that you might hurt yourself somehow."

"The fit lasted for several hours," Stefan added. "Harriet and I made sure there was nothing in your room that might hurt you – then we returned to the family room. Hoping you'd cry yourself to sleep."

"You carried on and carried on," Harriet said. "We were about to call Dr Harvey."

"I wanted to take you to hospital,"

interrupted Stefan.

"So what happened?" asked Amber. "How did it end?"

Again her parents silently consulted each other. Harriet seemed to non-verbally nudge Stefan to continue the story. But he shook his head, ever so slightly.

"Tell me!"

Harriet looked at Amber and forced herself to smile. "Let's just say that Dad and I soon discovered the best way for us all to get along was to give you lots of freedom – you needed plenty of room to make your own choices."

"Once we did that, it was plain sailing." Stefan punctuated the end of his story by placing his empty mug back on the tray.

Unable to get her parents to say much else, Amber finished her tea and went back to her room. Had she really seen a cautious look pass between them?

Amber moved to her window and peered out. She wasn't looking at anything in particular. Standing there, she could hear her parents having an intense discussion in Harriet's office. She couldn't make it out altogether, but it wasn't to do with their work. It was about her.

What's going on?

The telephone rang.

"What now?" Amber muttered, moving to answer it.

"Amber, it's me. Lori," a shaky voice said.

"Lori? What's the matter?"

"It's Brad, of course," Lori replied sadly.

"Honey, who's on the phone?" Amber's mother called from the other room.

Amber covered the mouthpiece and shouted back, "It's for me, Mom!" Then returning to Lori, she said, "What about Brad?"

"Maybe it's my fault," Lori said. "No, it's Brad's fault. I don't know – maybe it's no one's fault."

She was making very little sense. "Lori, slow down," Amber said. "Start at the beginning."

Amber heard Lori exhale a deep breath. "Oh, Amber, I've been seeing Brad again."

It took a moment for this to sink in. "You've been seeing Brad? Since you two broke up?"

"Yes," Lori said. "Isn't that stupid?"

Lori's voice became muddled, as if she had covered the mouthpiece and was talking to someone else at her house.

"Lori, who's there with you?" Amber asked.

"Elena," said Lori. "She sneaked out to be with me. I let her in the back door, so my parents wouldn't know."

"Who besides Elena and I know about Brad?" asked Amber.

"None of the other girls," Lori said. "I like Kayla and Jinx a lot, but you have to admit that they like to tease. So I didn't tell them."

"How often have you seen Brad?"

"A lot lately," Lori admitted. "But only on the sly. I sneak out at night and we go for a drive. Or I tell my parents I'm baby-sitting when I'm actually at Brad's. I ask him about Kristal, but he shrugs it off. It's totally stupid, I know. But I can't help it, Amber, I still love him."

"So what happened?" asked Amber.

"Well, earlier tonight I decided to sneak out and surprise him at his house," Lori reported. "I even went out and bought that new CD he wanted. I tapped on his bedroom window – but no one answered. I could hear voices, though, so I pulled myself up on the window ledge. And then I saw him and Kristal in his room, making out!"

"Lori, forget him," Amber advised. "Brad's no good. He's—"

Amber was interrupted by Elena taking the phone from Lori. "Amber, it's me, Elena," she said. "I think we should get Brad. He's a sleaze. He's just been using Lori."

"Get him?" Amber didn't like Elena's nasty tone. "What does that mean?"

"Teach him a lesson," Elena said firmly.

"Let's not be hasty," Amber replied. "Let's sleep on it and talk about it tomorrow."

There was a long pause. Finally Elena muttered, "Maybe you're right. But something has to be done about guys who think they can just use us."

Amber hung up the phone. As she got ready for bed, she thought about Brad and Lori, about Rachel and Troy – and most specifically about Christopher and herself.

Boys could be so cruel and selfish. Brad didn't seem to care that he was destroying Lori. He must have noticed that she'd been wasting away. How could he so blithely start up their relationship again? Didn't he know she'd be hurt? *What a jerk!*

Amber lay in bed but she found she couldn't sleep. Her mind was busy with fantasies of revenge. Maybe Elena was right.

There were a few decent guys, like Doug and

Joe. But maybe the Brads and Troys and Christophers of the world deserved what was coming to them.

CHAPTER TEN

A figure slept in a single bed in a room with posters of professional rodeo stars pinned on the wall. There were clothes slung over a chair. School books lay unopened on a desk. In the desk's top drawer were a pocket knife, a book of matches, mint flavoured toothpicks in paper wrappers, old baseball trading cards, and a shotgun cartridge loaded with buckshot. On the shelf were rodeo trophies and ribbons. A pair of grubby cowboy boots lay on their side on the carpeted floor. The curtains were closed. The room was dark and quiet.

Suddenly the bed covers were thrown back, as if by a cold gust of deadly wind, and the figure – a boy – was hurled to the floor.

He tried to get up, but the force of the wind knocked him down again. He grabbed the leg of the desk and pulled himself up – only to be thrown back hard against the wall.

The impact took his breath away. His mouth,

wide with terror, gasped for air.

Then the wind subsided. The boy caught his breath and rubbed his aching back. His knees were shaking, he wasn't ready to leave the support of the wall behind him.

Finally, he rushed to the bedroom window, determined to seal the window so this attack wouldn't happen again.

But, confused and horrified, he found the window had never been opened.

Then he heard something stir behind him. He was almost too terrified to turn round and see what it was. But the sound grew louder.

He turned and saw his heavy chest of drawers sliding across the floor. Faster and faster it approached him. Any path of escape was cut off.

The chest slammed him against the wall and pinned him to it. He heard something inside him crack. He tasted blood in his mouth.

He cried out in horrible pain.

So did Amber.

She found herself sitting up in bed, drenched in sweat. Her breathing was intense; her heart was racing. *Did I scream? I must have.*

The dream of the boy getting hurt was so vivid. She tried to replay it in her mind. Was it a dream – or some kind of psychic vision? Was it all in her head – or had she somehow been a witness to a real life event?

She concentrated on seeing the boy's face.

Blond hair, thin face. Brown eyes.

Nice looking – when he wasn't terrified.

Amber squeezed her eyes closed, concentrating even harder on the mental image.

A familiar face.

A famous face?

No. Familiar in her day-to-day life.

"God," she whispered, "it's Brad. He's hurt!"

Amber hopped out of bed and pulled on her jeans. *I have to help him!* She tucked her nightshirt into the jeans before buttoning them up, grabbed her shoes from under the bed and put them on without bothering with socks. She found her glasses next to her bedside clock.

It was three in the morning.

It had to be a dream, she reasoned. He couldn't be hurt.

Could he?

Now Amber was wide awake. She could either get undressed again and kid herself that she'd be able to sleep. Or she could sneak out and find out if anything had actually happened.

"I'll never sleep, not knowing," she told herself. So Amber crept through the house, took her truck keys from the kitchen counter, and woke Patsy.

"Come on, girl," Amber whispered. "I'm feeling pretty freaked. I could use some company."

The old dog yawned, stretched her limbs, got to her feet and shook out her fur.

Amber opened the truck door and Patsy jumped inside, then Amber jumped in and put on her seat belt. Releasing the parking brake she let the truck roll down the driveway. At the bottom she started the engine and pointed the pickup in the direction of Brad's house.

At this hour, the streets of Los Alamos were empty. Homes were dark, except for porch lights. Businesses were closed, except for a few all-night fast-food restaurants.

Amber had been to Brad's house for a party, back when he and Lori were together, so she had no problem finding it tucked away in a large housing development.

"I'll just drive by his house," she told Patsy, "and make sure everything's fine."

But, as they approached, it was evident to Amber that everything was *not* fine.

As she neared his block she could see blue lights flashing on the neighbouring houses. Stopping at the corner, she leant over the steering wheel for a better view.

Several police cars were parked at Brad's house.

"Oh no!" Amber muttered.

She put the pick-up in reverse and backed out of sight. Then she slowly turned it round and headed back towards home.

"It wasn't a dream!" she told herself. "It really happened!"

But had she actually caused it to happen – or did she just watch it happen in her psychic visit? Had Lori made it happen, and Amber had somehow tapped into the weird energy?

A sharp pain shot through Amber's body and she had to pull the car over. The dark knot was about to possess her. But this time she was able to push it back into its unknown place deep inside her.

"Patsy," she told her dog, "we're really in trouble now."

Amber gunned the truck engine. She desperately needed to get home before something else could happen.

Mentally exhausted, she pulled the truck into

the driveway and crept inside.

"Thanks for coming, Patsy," she whispered as the dog returned to her bed in the utility room. "Luckily, you can't tell anyone what's going on."

Back in her bed, Amber tossed and turned for what seemed like hours. She was the one who had first got her friends into this mess. How was she going to stop it before it got totally out of control?

Earlier, her parents had told her she'd always had a mind of her own. Maybe she and the other girls could use their collective mental energy to rid themselves of this uncontrollable force.

This hopeful thought brought with it the possibility of sleep. Amber forced herself to think other positive thoughts. How much she loved the desert. How great it was to have friends like Jinx, Kayla, Lori, and Elena. How understanding her parents were. What an interesting place New Mexico was to live. How much she loved riding her mustang.

But, try as she might, these thoughts began to sour. Maybe the desert was poisoned with radiation that was causing LASSO's unwieldy power. Maybe her friends were all liars – after all, someone had spilled the beans about the group's amazing feats. What information were her parents being so careful to hide from her? And riding – the last time at the ranch, she and Chris had had that awful scene.

Chris.

Boys.

Brad and Troy.

Half asleep and half awake, she saw that image of Troy Evans in the parking lot. Laughing at poor Rachel. And it made her angry all over again.

In her mind she replayed what LASSO had done to Troy. How they'd thrown him against another car and scared him silly. But this time she imagined him smashing ever harder against that other car. This time Troy didn't get up off the ground. Instead, he stayed there, rolling in pain. Holding his arm which hung in pieces like a torn ribbon from his shoulder.

Weirdly, this fantasy of revenge brought a smile to Amber's sleeping face. And somewhere, deep in the recesses of her being, she heard the chant, "I've got the power! I've got the power!"

Even asleep, Amber felt something struggling to take control of her mind. A strange though not altogether unpleasant magnet pulling at it. Still, something told her not to lose herself to this ominous, faceless authority.

"No," she muttered. "You won't control me."

She fought and fought. Her limbs became twisted in her bed sheets and blanket, but she continued to struggle against the invisible force.

"NO!" she shouted, violently flailing her arms, beating away whatever was invading her sleep. "I said *NO*!"

She felt like an animal fighting its way out of a cage. Either she escaped, or she'd be trapped for ever.

"I mean it!" Now awake, Amber forced her mind to remember stupid things – like the names of all the kids in her second grade class, the contents of the refrigerator, multiplication and division tables – anything to create a field of mental resistance.

Finally she sensed herself getting the upper hand.

Strangely, as quickly as it had first attacked her, the threat began to retreat.

Relieved, Amber burst into tears and curled up into a foetal position. She hugged her knees and told herself over and over, "It's all right. It's all over. We won."

CHAPTER ELEVEN

*Your fierce little temper comes from that natal
Mars in Scorpio. Your forceful drive is too
much for your friends. This is a time to work
solo. Try to remain objective.*

"**D**id you hear? Troy was thrown out of bed
last night and got his arm broken in three
places," Jinx reported to Amber in a whisper at
her locker the next morning.

Amber was stunned at how quickly word had
got round.

"That's not all," added Jinx. "Something
weird happened at Brad's house last night, too."

"What?"

"He's not talking about it – he's too scared,"
Jinx said. "But his ribs are taped. Two of them
are cracked. The rodeo's tomorrow night! How
are we going to compete with Troy and Brad
out?"

Although there were plenty of students in the

hall between classes, the girls easily heard Elena rushing up to join them. "Did you hear that Troy and Brad's injuries may keep them out of the rodeo!" she moaned. "That's terrible! The school really needs them to win the title."

"Will you shut up about that stupid rodeo?" Amber said in a harsh whisper.

"Look, don't yell at me," Elena shot back. "I'm not the one who's been having secret meetings and not calling everyone."

"What does that mean?" Amber asked.

"Did you guys meet without me?" Elena demanded. "Because that's pretty low."

"Meeting?" Jinx gasped. "Since when was there a meeting? Nobody called me."

"There was no meeting," Amber shouted over the two of them. "And for your information, last night I was home alone."

"I was with Lori," Elena said, "but then I had to leave."

"Do you think Lori could have hurt Brad on her own?" Jinx asked.

Amber shrugged. "I don't know. She sure was mad at him last night. She was ready to kill him."

The girls stopped, realizing the school halls were unusually quiet. Many students were milling round, trying to listen to their conversation.

"Look," hissed Elena. "We're becoming geeks! Everyone hates us!"

Doug Farber broke from the passive crowd and approached them. "Hey, Jinx," he said, nervously tugging at one earlobe. "I'm sorry if I embarrassed you in front of your friends the other day at lunch." He chuckled and shrugged. "Hey, I know a girl like you wouldn't be interested in a guy like me."

"Doug, what's going on?" Jinx said, pulling him towards the lockers. "You don't owe me an apology."

"You consider me your friend," he continued. "Don't you?"

"Of course." Jinx put both hands on her hips. "Doug, you're acting very, very weird."

"No," he ventured with a lopsided grin. "Just cautious."

"Cautious?" Jinx repeated. Then she made a face. "Doug, are you afraid of us?"

"Why would anyone be afraid of you guys? Catch you later." Doug disappeared back into the swarm of students heading for their next class.

"You guys," Jinx said as she rejoined their

circle, "my friend Doug is afraid of us."

Amber nodded. "Yeah, and I don't like it."

Elena shot a glance over her shoulder and whispered, "Everyone is being super nice to me, as if I'm going to turn them all into toads. I've sold more rodeo tickets than anyone in the Pep Club. Girls have been offering to give me their sales."

Amber's head throbbed and giant waves of heat were washing over her. The news of Troy's broken arm and Brad's injuries frightened her. She pretended to head for class, but then hurried into the girls' toilet. She felt like throwing up.

At the sink she wet a paper towel and pressed it to her forehead. *This is insane*, she thought.

Amber stared at her frightened reflection in the mirror, waiting for the class bell to ring. When she was certain that the halls were empty, she finally left the toilet and headed for the front doors. *Air. I need some fresh air.*

But no sooner did she step outside than Christopher rushed up from behind and confronted her. "Am I next?" he boldly asked.

"Were you following me?" Amber demanded.

"No...yes," Chris admitted. "Answer my question. Am I next?"

"I don't know," Amber shot back. "But if you know what's good for you – stay out of my head!"

With a worried look, Chris retreated inside. Amber saw him glance nervously over his shoulder, as if somehow she might send a deadly object into his back.

I can't be here today. This is too much to handle.

But Amber didn't want to be alone, either. So she crept along the outside of the school, past Lori's classroom window.

Catching the eye of one of Lori's classmates, Amber signalled to him to get Lori's attention. He did, and Lori glanced outside, surprised to see Amber.

"What?" mouthed Lori.

"I need you," whispered Amber. "Meet me at my truck."

Amber watched as Lori raised her hand, made an excuse about not feeling well, and left the classroom.

The girls joined up at Amber's truck.

"Amber, you look awful," observed Lori. "Are you sick?"

"I don't know," Amber honestly replied. "My life's a wreck. I'm not sleeping. Not eating. All this tension about LASSO is really gnawing my insides. Everyone's looking at me as if everything bad that's happened is my fault."

"I know what you mean," Lori said. "It's like people think we're evil spirits incarnate."

"Lori?" Amber stared into her friend's eyes. "Did you have anything to do with Brad's...accident?"

"I must have," Lori said with a shrug. "We all must have. Don't you think?"

"I don't know," admitted Amber.

"But I was asleep when it happened," Lori added.

"So was I," replied Amber.

"This is all getting too weird," said Lori.

"It's frightening," said Amber, hugging her friend. "I wonder if somehow we all joined up in our sleep. It sounds bizarre – but there has to be some explanation for what happened."

"You sound like your parents," Lori half mocked. "To a scientist, everything must have an explanation."

"If we could discover what causes this force, maybe we can undo it," Amber said. "I say we go to the library. They have several books on telekinesis. I think one is even called *Strange Powers of the Mind*."

"Beats sitting through French," Lori said with a smile.

As the two girls drove to the main branch of the Los Alamos Public Library, Lori chattered on about the rodeo scheduled for tomorrow evening. "Knowing Brad," she said, "he'll get up on his horse, cracked ribs and all, and win first place."

But Amber wasn't listening. Instead, she was seized by the dark knot returning inside her. And growing ever bigger.

At the library, the girls keyed in several different subjects – telekinesis, Uri Geller, occult, psychokinesis, witchcraft – into the computer. It turned up dozens of related titles in the library collection. The girls went to the shelves and removed the appropriate books, bringing them to a table in a private research room.

For the rest of the afternoon they pored through the volumes.

"Oooh, this is creepy," Lori reported, holding up a thick book on the occult.

"What?" asked Amber.

"The witches of Salem, Massachusetts," Lori said. "Listen. 'In 1692, two young girls reported to authorities that they had been recruited by a large coven of witches. The girls said the adult witches could put spells on people and nature and make strange things happen. Over a hundred people were arrested in the ensuing hysteria, and nineteen were burnt as witches.'"

"We're not witches," Amber reminded her friend.

"How can you be sure?" Lori whispered with panic in her voice. "The local Indians believe in a spirit world, in shamans who can tap magic powers."

"Lori, this is the end of the twentieth century," Amber said. "The Salem witch hunt was over three hundred years ago. Before Benjamin Franklin's crude experiments with electricity." She showed Lori an entry in the encyclopaedia. "Look at this entry about X-rays. They were discovered by Wilhelm Roentgen in 1895. And look – technology's gadgets, from the television to the microwave oven, are all sources of potentially dangerous radiation. A man working on the military's distant early warning radar system was killed by the microwave radiation produced in the system. Although there wasn't a scratch on his body, the autopsy revealed that his internal organs had been literally cooked."

"Gross!" Lori said. "But what does radiation have to do with LASSO?"

Amber picked up a different book. "This is a study of Uri Geller," she said. "'The force of electromagnetism combines electric and magnetic fields. It gives off electromagnetic radiation which travels at the speed of light — 186,000 miles or 300,000 kilometres per second. X-rays and gamma-rays are kinds of electromagnetic radiation.'"

"I don't get your point," said a confused Lori.

"Listen to this." Amber read on. "'Electromagnetism is the most likely explanation for the Geller phenomena. The brain of a telekinetic person would send off concentrated electromagnetic waves, which, in turn, could cause the mutation — or change — in the object being focused upon.' Like a metal spoon."

"Or a table or dog," Lori added. "But I thought radiation was bad."

"It can be good, bad, or neutral," Amber

151

explained. "Take the sun. Some of the sun's radiation – heat and light – is essential to life. But some of its radiation – ultraviolet, for example – can cause sunburn or, worse, cancer."

"I still don't get this," Lori said. "I just don't understand how the five of us made it work."

Amber turned to another article she had marked with a paper clip. "This is about how girls and women who live together start affecting one another. 'It is not unusual for female roommates to find that, over a short time, their menstrual periods have moved together into one household cycle.' Meaning that they start their periods on the same day."

"OK," Lori said. "That might explain how five close friends might – I say, might – start focusing their power as one. What else?"

Amber opened a psychology book to a page she had marked with a scrap of paper. "It says here that people have purportedly visited each other in their dreams." She handed the passage to Lori.

"So?" asked an increasingly sceptical Lori.

"So, maybe the five of us dreamed about Troy and Brad getting hurt – and it happened!" said Amber, frustrated with Lori's attitude.

Lori shook her head. "Amber, are you saying that we all joined minds in our dreams and focused our energy on another person?"

"It's possible," Amber said.

"It doesn't say it's possible in anything you've shown me," Lori said. "That's wishful thinking on your part."

"It's not wishful thinking," Amber protested. "I'm putting out a bunch of theoretical possibilities. Stating hypotheses is part of the scientific process. If you'd paid attention in school instead of worrying about a jerk like Brad, you'd know exactly what I'm doing here."

"What you're doing," Lori shot back, "is trying to force a square peg into a round hole. Spare me, but you're not being a scientist! And take back what you said about Brad!"

"Why should I?" Amber said in a loud whisper. "It's true. You're here to avoid French, not to get to the bottom of—"

"Get off your high horse!" Lori interrupted. "You're not my friend! You're jealous because, while it lasted, Brad and I had a real relationship. Not like you and Chris. He never loved you. He only liked that you had a truck and—"

"Drop dead, Lori!" Amber said.

"Right after you!" Lori shot back. "None of us would be in this situation if it weren't for you!"

"What does that mean?" Amber asked.

"Oh, is your scientific brain failing you, Einstein?" asked Lori sarcastically. "Who first told us about bending a spoon? Who hosted the slumber party? Who got us to lift that boulder in the park? You, Amber! You!"

"But you were the one who wanted to direct the power against Kristal," Amber said in her own defence. "I never planned to use the power on a person."

"Well, you didn't hesitate for a second when Elena suggested it," Lori shot back.

"And it was you, wasn't it, that told everyone at school about LASSO?" Amber demanded.

"What if I did?" Lori spat the words at Amber.

"Don't you understand what you've done?" Amber shouted. "Our lives will never be the same. You ruined everything."

Amber was so angry with Lori and frustrated at the whole business that she raised the book over her head, tempted to hurl it at her friend.

The action caused Lori to back down in fear. "Hey, Amber, get a hold of yourself," she said. "I didn't mean it. We were only letting off steam. I'm sorry if you—"

She was interrupted when the book suddenly leapt from Amber's hand and rocketed across the room. It hit the wall with a bang before dropping like a stone to the ground.

"Did you do that?" Amber asked Lori.

"No, I swear," Lori replied. "I thought you did."

"This is creepy," Amber said, her voice quivering. "Very creepy."

"You're scaring me," Lori whispered with tears spilling down her cheeks. "Amber, you're really scaring me."

"It wasn't me," Amber insisted.

"It *was* you," insisted Lori.

Amber looked at her friend. She was ready to deny Lori's accusation. Sure, she had to watch her thoughts and learn to control her temper. But this power couldn't belong just to her.

"It's you, Amber," Lori said, moving to the door. "You know it, and I know it."

After Lori left, Amber glanced down at her shaking hands. "I've got the power," she chanted, frightened and anxious. "I've got the power."

CHAPTER TWELVE

There is an acute conjunction between
Neptune and Uranus which will cause events
to happen with a fierce suddenness. These
events, will be shrouded in mystery. But this
too shall pass because these two planets will
not meet up again for another 174 years!

Friday was spent preparing for that evening's
All-Conference Rodeo. A lot of kids skipped
school – some for valid reasons, many not – so
Amber's absence was hardly noticed.

She had suffered a horrible night. After the
fight with Lori in the library, she had told her
parents she didn't feel well and stayed in her
room. When her friends called on the phone,
Amber insisted she didn't want to talk to
anybody.

She had stayed up all night watching TV,
drinking strong tea, splashing ice water on her
face, anything to prevent herself from falling

157

asleep. She was afraid of what might happen if she did.

In the morning Amber was a wreck, physically exhausted and mentally on edge. Alienated from her friends, fearing for her sanity, she stood bleary-eyed in the doorway of her parents' home office and asked, "What's wrong with me?"

Harriet and Stefan looked at her appearance in dismay, and then at each other. Stefan gave Harriet a short nod, then she turned to Amber and said, "It's time."

Her parents put Amber in the car and headed out of Los Alamos. They weren't heading towards Santa Fe or Albuquerque, the two largest cities in New Mexico. Instead Stefan turned the car east into the desert.

"Where are you taking me?" Amber asked.

"You'll see," Harriet said. "Be patient."

"But Mom—"

"We'll be there in a little more than two hours," Stefan assured her.

At an unmarked exit, they left the highway and went down a dirt road. The road was deeply rutted, and Stefan had to slow down to a crawl. The landscape became more and more desolate. All vegetation disappeared except for a scattered cactus or two. The soil became nothing but red-tinted rock. The sun beat down on the car, causing Harriet to turn on the air-conditioning.

Usually when out for a drive, Amber's parents liked to listen to classical music. But today the cassette player and radio were off. All Amber could hear was the whine of the engine and the harsh spin of the tyres against the gravel road as they ate up the miles.

Finally, they arrived at a deserted town located at the base of some bare rocky bluffs. From the look of it, the ghost town had once been a prosperous settlement. There were several large warehouse-looking buildings, and rows and rows of breeze block houses, all of which now had roofs that had caved in and their windows blown out. Weeds had conquered what looked liked former streets and driveways.

"Is it safe to get out?" Amber asked.

"Yes," Stefan said, before adding, "for a quick visit."

Amber got out of the car. There was an odd sadness to the place, which had obviously been abandoned years before. It seemed like the set for a horror movie about some awful creature which had terrorized a small, isolated town, killing everyone in it.

"What is this place?" she asked.

"Believe it or not," Harriet said, "it's where you were born."

"No way!" protested Amber. "I was born in Los Alamos."

"I'm sorry," Stefan said. "We lied about that."

"Lied?" repeated Amber. "Why?"

"To protect you," he said.

"Protect me?" Amber echoed. "From what?"

"Come," Harriet said, avoiding an answer. "Let me show you the house."

The three walked along a row of houses left to nature. They could see animal droppings, tiny skeletons, and other evidence that the only inhabitants now were hawks, snakes and prairie dogs.

"Mom, this is kind of spooky," Amber said.

"It didn't used to be," Harriet said. "Eighteen years ago, it was a buzz of activity – believe it or not."

"There." Stefan pointed to a house. The weathered door dangled against the outer wall from one hinge, and Amber could see weeds pushing up through what was left of the living

160

room floor. "That's where we lived."

"I never expected to deliver you at home," Harriet said. "We planned to have the baby in a regular hospital, in Los Alamos. But I went into labour early and..."

"I was born out here?" said Amber, her jaw about to drop. "In the middle of nowhere?"

"It was remote," Stefan corrected, "but hardly nowhere. We had a store, a gas station, a research centre, a health clinic. Even a one-room school."

"But what were you doing here in the first place?" Amber asked.

Her parents looked at her for a moment. Then her mother said, "Amber, please understand. We were both working on a secret government project. We had to swear oaths of secrecy."

Amber nodded. "What secret project?"

Stefan began to explain. "The government chose this site because it was already off-limits to the general public—because of some uranium mines located over those hills." He pointed further east. Amber shielded her eyes from the sun for a look. "They're gone now, the mines, but in the 1950s and 60s, they were a rich source of U-235, a naturally occurring radioactive isotope of uranium."

"To be used in bombs?" asked Amber.

"Weapons, and many other things," answered Harriet. "Nuclear power plants, for instance. And medical purposes, like X-rays and radiation therapy."

"Harriet and I were part of a team attempting to come up with a development of what we call the CAT scan," Stefan said. "The official term for the process is Computerized Axial Tomography."

"I've heard of CAT scans," Amber said. "It's what doctors use to check for brain tumours. It's like a better form of X-ray, right? It produces a more detailed image."

Harriet nodded. "One that's much more precise than the old standard X-ray," she said. "Well, Stefan and I were part of a team assigned to develop this technology further. All of us were excited at the possibilities. We believed we would change the face of modern medicine – and we did. But we also discovered the power of this energy we had unleashed."

"Worse yet," Stefan added, "we learnt that the government's plans were not only for peaceful applications. No, they were using our research to help develop better counterintelligence weapons. Imagine, for instance, a spy satellite in space that could disrupt, even destroy a sophisticated communications system simply by pinpointing a minute, incredibly intense beam of radiation at it."

"So you moved from this town?" Amber asked. "Because you didn't like what the government was doing?"

"That, and because we were increasingly worried about you," Harriet said.

"Me?"

"The longer we stayed here, the worse things got," Harriet continued. "Children were starting to be born with defects. Irregular heart valves, shuffled organs, nerve damage – that sort of thing. At a rate far too high for such a small area. Animals, too, were affected. A rancher living not five miles away reported a lamb born with two heads. Oh, it made all the newspapers."

"People drove from all over to see the curiosity." Stefan took up the story. "Everyone thought it was an amusing freak of nature – but we knew better. We knew it had to be caused by the unique electromagnetic fields generated by our own research, combined with the residual radiation from the nearby mines."

"I think we were all contaminated," Harriet confessed. "My problem pregnancies were a result of it."

"And – it's a silly example, I know – but I still can't wear a quartz-powered watch," Stefan added. "To this day, something inside me literally stops time!"

"Wait a second," Amber said. The flood of information was overwhelming. "You're saying between being exposed to the radioactivity from the mines and the electromagnetic research, that we were all contaminated?"

Harriet nodded sadly. "Finally, everyone on the research team attended a secret meeting at our house. I remember, we went round all the people in the living room and not a single family lacked a health concern or weird experience to share. It became obvious that we hadn't been properly warned of the risks of working here. Or, I should say, no one ever dreamed that our work might create such hazards." She shook her head in dismay. "Somehow we had created – I don't know how to put it, a monster. People were angry and very, very frightened."

"We talked about you, Amber," Stefan said. "Our small daughter who had the power to move objects."

"So it's true," Amber said. "I *was* moving my toys and puzzles just by thinking about them."

Harriet nodded. "Your power wasn't evident until you were three years old. And then, it was erratic – sometimes there, sometimes not."

"It seemed to come most often when you were angry," Stefan said. "And it could get quite ugly."

"We soon realized that, being so young, you had no idea of your terrible power," Harriet continued. "Remember the other night when we were talking about your working on that jigsaw puzzle when I told you it was bedtime?"

Amber nodded.

"I'll never forget it," Stefan cut in. "This tiny three-year-old exploding with anger. Then the puzzle pieces lifting off the ground and spinning in a circle. Faster and faster the puzzle pieces flew, powered by an unknown force. Like a tornado!"

"The pieces knocked over the lamp," Harriet remembered. "Knocked pictures off the wall. Dad and I had to duck for cover! It was like a tornado destroying everything in its path. Out of control, you unleashed a force with the destructive power of the atom. That's when we decided our main concern was to keep you happy."

"This explains how telekinesis could happen," Amber whispered in awe.

Her parents looked at each other. "I don't know if it quite explains it," Harriet said. "But it does prove that it's possible."

"Once we moved back to Los Alamos, we thought it – the power – was gone," Stefan said. "You showed every sign of growing up a normal, if unusually bright child." Then he sighed. "But it seems that it's come back."

"It's like a dark knot inside my head," Amber tried to explain. "I get angry and then boom, something happens."

Harriet touched Amber's arm. "It's time to get you some expert help at controlling your anger. This power is an extremely dangerous gift."

"Do you think my friends have the same condition?" Amber asked.

Her parents exchanged a look. "It's possible for some of your friends to have the same power," Stefan said. "Kayla's father has been with the lab for sixteen years."

"We can't know how many other kids were

affected," said Harriet, putting her arm round Amber. "Many things happened at that time. So much unseen power was unleashed in the early years of research. Terrible, horrifying power. It could have affected more children than just you. But," she added with a sad smile, "it's you that we worry about."

"Being here is making me quite sad and anxious," Stefan confessed. "Amber, any other questions?"

She shook her head. Her head that was filled with its own sadness and fear. "This place gives me the creeps," she said.

"Me, too," said Harriet. "Let's get out of here."

As they drove out of the research town, Amber noticed a child's tricycle wrapped round a piñon tree. Wrapped in such a way that only some incredibly strong force could have bent it that way. Beside it was a crumpled red wagon and a twisted pogo stick. Even a small rusting shovel was embedded in the base of the tree,

Did I do that? she wondered.

All the way home, her parents' words describing her telekinetic power echoed in Amber's mind. "...a force with the destructive power of the atom." Amber had seen photographs of the unspeakable devastation at Hiroshima and Nagasaki. If a three-year-old could tap into that kind of energy, imagine what five eighteen-year-olds could do. The horrible possibilities made her shudder.

It was late afternoon by the time the Moyers pulled into their driveway. Amber saw a note taped to the front door.

As her parents parked in the garage and went inside, Amber ran round to the front to retrieve the note, which read:

> Amber — We're off to the Rodeo. We're joining forces to win big for LA West. We're number one, and in a few hours everyone will know it! Meet us there.
>
> Jinx and all.

"Oh, no," Amber groaned. "I've got to stop them!"

CHAPTER THIRTEEN

Amber ran to her room, grabbed her rodeo ticket, and raced back outside. She jumped into her pick-up and backed out of the driveway.

Her mother came rushing out of the house. "Amber, where are you going?"

"To the rodeo," Amber shouted back, putting the truck into first gear.

"The rodeo? Why?" her mother called.

"No time to explain!" Amber shot back.

"Amber!" Harriet screamed.

But it was too late. The truck was speeding down the block. At the corner Amber didn't obey the stop sign and nearly knocked a kid off his bike.

Not stopping to see if he was all right, Amber drove like a madwoman through the normally quiet streets of Los Alamos. She honked while approaching every intersection, then sped through it without a second thought. Forgetting which streets were one way, she turned into oncoming traffic and nearly crashed into another car.

"Hey, you crazy kid!" the driver of the other car shouted. "Who taught you how to drive?"

"Sorry!" Amber yelled back. Still she didn't slow down. She floored the accelerator, passing slower cars left and right. She was afraid of being stopped by a traffic cop and arrested for reckless driving. But she was more afraid of not getting to the rodeo before her friends did something terrible.

She raced into the parking lot at the county showground. The field was jammed with cars, trucks, Jeeps, and livestock trailers. Kids with numbers pinned to their backs were walking round in cowboy hats and leather chaps. Others were leading horses towards the rodeo arena.

If she had stopped to notice, the crowd looked dressed for a country music concert. Some of the guys were wearing duster coats and fancy belt buckles. Girls were dressed in tight leather skirts and embroidered jean jackets. But all that Amber keyed in on were the covered grandstands looming ahead.

"Ladies and gentlemen, boys and girls, please take your seats," she heard the announcer boom over the loudspeakers. "The

Grand Parade which starts our All-Conference Rodeo is about to begin!"

Amber pushed her way past a team from another school performing their roping warm-ups. She narrowly avoided being snared by one of the flying lassos.

Ahead, she could see rodeo workers herding calves into wooden pens to await the roping events. Others were arranging the heavy oil drums used for the barrel racing competition on the dirt infield.

She tore off the stub and slapped the rest of her ticket into the hand of a gate attendant and raced past. Pushing and shoving, Amber worked her way through the crowd milling towards the aisle leading up to the grandstand seats.

"Excuse me," she shouted. "Coming through! Emergency!"

At the top of the grandstand, she scanned the seats for her friends. "Where are they?" Amber whispered. She looked and looked again, increasingly worried that they might be hiding themselves.

"There!" Finally, she spotted them in the front row box seats, reserved only for VIPs. They were all holding hands. There was a ring of vacant seats all round the box. Obviously, everyone was afraid to sit near them.

"Oh no," Amber whispered, "what could they do? Hurt the riders from the other school? Injure the horses? I have got to stop them!"

She began to charge down the stairs, but an usher stopped her. "Miss, may I see your ticket?" he asked.

"I'm sitting with my friends," said an annoyed Amber, handing him the stub. "Down there!"

"Not according to this ticket you aren't," he said, shaking his head. "You're in the general admission area. That's at the top of the grandstands."

"Leave it to Elena to mess up," said Amber. "Please, then," she asked the usher, "can't I just go down and talk to my friends."

"Sorry, no," he said. "Our instructions are to keep the aisles clear."

"But this is an emergency!" insisted Amber.

"It always is," the usher replied snootily. "If I let you go down there, what's to stop anyone else who claims they have friends in the front row?"

"Fine!" Amber snapped, taking back the ticket stub.

She turned and charged up the stairs, determined to find another way to reach her friends.

"Ladies and gentlemen, boys and girls," the announcer boomed, "please stand for the presentation of the colours."

Behind her she heard western music pumped over the showground's loudspeakers, as the Grand Parade began. A rider from Los Alamos led the parade, proudly waving the American flag. Just behind her was a boy waving the state flag of New Mexico. Riders from each school in the conference galloped in, holding his or her school flag in one hand. The spectators responded with a loud cheer.

Amber worked her way back through the crowd, towards the south entrance near the refreshment stand. She was almost to the right entrance when she spotted Christopher.

She was going to approach him and explain – but then she noticed he was busy talking to someone else. Emily, the blonde from the ranch. He was handing her a soft drink and a big cone of candyfloss. As he did, she leant into him, nuzzling his shoulder with her cheek.

Amber's vision blurred and she literally saw red. Red in Emily's flirting. Red in

Christopher's betrayal. Red in her own jealousy.

Amber spun round to avoid seeing any more. The dark knot inside her tightened and she grabbed the back of her neck in pain. Anger consumed her, as if the knot had dripped a poisonous ink that spread to every cell of her being.

Stumbling forward, she saw Brad hitching up his cowboy shirt and proudly showing his bandaged ribs to Kristal Taylor. Kristal seemed to coo at Brad's bravery for competing with such an injury.

Thoughts of Lori's haunted eyes, ringed with the lingering hurt of Brad's betrayal, came to Amber. Although the two of them had left on awkward terms, Amber felt for her friend, who had practically starved herself to death just to get Brad's attention.

Amber's mind spun dizzily. Why were people so cruel and thoughtless? Why did boys insist on taking everything from girls, including their dignity? *What did this stupid rodeo mean, anyway, except the right to claim the high school championship of a small city in an underpopulated state in this vast wasteland called the American West?*

Amber suddenly forgot about trying to reach her friends. Instead, she moved in a slow circle, like a movie camera doing a 360-degree turn. In a whirl she saw pockets of students enjoying themselves, laughing, totally unaware of how stupid and insignificant they were. Laughing at everyone but themselves. Not caring about other people's feelings.

Amber got angry. Angrier than she'd ever been.

Someone bumped into her. "Hey, girl, you're blocking the way," a beefy boy with a bad complexion bellowed. "Move your butt!"

"First off, I'm not your 'girl'." Amber spun slowly, focusing her hatred on the boy. "And second, why don't you—"

"Drop dead, you ugly cow!" the boy cut in. "Now get out of my way!"

"No!" Amber screamed. "You get out of *my* way! All of you!"

She waved her hands in front of her eyes, as if trying to scrub the entire rodeo crowd from her vision.

A low rumble began deep beneath the grandstands.

The boy, seeing the expression on her face, stumbled backwards.

Amber turned again, bumping into another kid from school who she didn't like. The crowd round the refreshment stand parted swiftly as Amber got more and more angry. Students from her school were warning perfect strangers to "stay out of that girl's way, she's evil." Spectators began to leave their seats, to see what the fuss was about.

"I hate you!" rasped Amber. "I hate all of you!"

Through blurred vision, Amber saw her horrified friends trying to push their way through the crowd. They were calling her name over and over.

Amber spun round and round. Every face she saw returned a look of fear and disgust.

She tried to stem her own anger – but it was out of control. The dark knot tightened harder and harder until it was transformed into a black tornado of fury.

"Oh my god!" someone screamed.

"I don't believe it!" another yelled in panic.

"Run! Run! It's coming loose!" a third warned.

Amber slowly raised her head. The massive grandstand roof was freeing itself from its pillars, bolt by screeching bolt.

"It's going to crash!"

Terrified screams filled the air, but Amber didn't let up. She couldn't.

"We're all going to die!"

The support beams pulled themselves up and off their concrete anchors. The sound was horrible – like a machine gun spitting bullets. Metal ripped apart. Rock and cement snapped into millions of pieces.

The grandstand roof rose and hovered above the panic-stricken crowd, then collapsed on top of them, pinning hundreds of spectators beneath it.

Amber staggered backwards. All round her was chaos as people outside the grandstand tried to flee the arena. Several kids struggled to keep from being trampled. Scores were injured.

Ambulance crews, which had been relaxing and waiting for the rodeo, sprang into action.

"Call the fire department!" a paramedic shouted.

"Get as many paramedics here as you can!" a police officer shouted into her portable radio.

Amber froze. People were pushing her in the back, trying to get clear of the disaster. Horses reared up and neighed, and snapped free of their reins. The frightened beasts began to gallop haphazardly as if trapped in a lightning storm. Others, still stuck in pens, kicked and kicked until the wooden slants splintered, freeing them to join the mêlée.

"Stampede!" someone yelled. "Stampede!"

Not looking, Amber stumbled forward, crashing headlong into her parents, who had followed her to the showground.

"Amber!" her mother screamed, taking her by the wrists.

Pale and sobbing, Amber collapsed against Harriet. "They did this!" she cried. "Look what they did!"

"Amber, look at me!" Harriet insisted, pulling on Amber's wrists. "Look at me!"

Amber's hysterical face tried to focus on her mother.

"This is no 'they'," Harriet told her. "It's only you. You did this, Amber. You did this!"

Amber turned to her father. "Daddy," she said, her body shaking, "it wasn't my fault!"

"Maybe you can't help it," Stefan said, his own voice quivering, "but it was your fault. You are responsible."

"You both hate me!" Amber cried. "Everybody hates me!"

"Amber! Amber!" Harriet shook her hard.

Amber crumpled, and Harriet and Stefan had to lift her to her feet. "I'm sorry, Amber," Harriet said, as they pulled her to a safe spot. "But you have to listen. You must. Oh my god, why didn't we tell her before?"

Stefan bent forwards putting his face in front of hers. "Amber, that parents meeting we told you about," he said, loud enough to be heard above the din, "was all about you. Other parents told stories about what happened when you were with their kids."

Amber squeezed her eyes shut and opened them, trying to focus.

"Amber, please listen," Harriet urged. The sheer panic in her voice was almost palpable. "It's important."

For the first time since the roof blew off, Amber felt her feet underneath her. "I'm listening," she said in a small shaky voice.

"Amber," Stefan continued, "the other families were frightened of you."

"Of me?" Amber echoed. "Why?"

"You were hurting their children when you got angry," Stefan explained. "You were the only one with this strange power. Do you understand? The only one!"

"Amber, listen to us," Harriet said with tears

in her eyes. "We can't protect you any longer. You are the only one who can stop this."

"But I can't!" stormed Amber. "It's too powerful for me to stop! You don't understand!"

"Amber, please!" shouted Stefan. "People are hurt. Trapped and scared. Use the power to help them. You have to do this now. You have the power."

CHAPTER FOURTEEN

Amber turned and witnessed the terrible scene she had created. The roof lay in shambles, scattered over the front bench seats into the infield. Pinned spectators were screaming in pain. Emergency crews were frantically trying to move massive slabs of metal and pipe.

"Help them," Harriet urged.

Amber nodded. With all her mental strength she focused on the roof.

But nothing happened. "It's not working!" she told her parents.

"Don't tap your anger," Stefan advised. "Tap all the goodness inside you."

"But the goodness doesn't work," protested Amber.

"Try!" Harriet insisted. "Summon all the positive energy you have."

Amber tried, really tried. She envisioned the happy ending – people saved, no one killed or seriously injured.

But again, the roof failed to move.

"I can't do it alone!" she moaned.

"You're not alone," Kayla said, appearing behind her and taking her hand. "Come on, girlfriend, people need you!"

"Yes, Amber, try," Lori pleaded, taking Amber's other hand. "Please try! Brad's missing! I don't care about Kristal and him. She can have Brad. I just want him safe!"

"Hurry, Amber," added Jinx, stepping into the circle. "You've got the power."

"We're here with you," Elena said, completing the fivesome.

The girls joined hands with Harriet and Stefan. Amber tried to focus, but grew scared. *What if I can't do it?*

Suddenly a hand touched her elbow. Turning round, she saw Christopher, a deep gash on his forehead.

"Use your power to save our friends," he whispered in her ear. "I'll help. I'll focus with you."

Amber studied Christopher's eyes. He looked back, not breaking his gaze. He was no longer frightened to look at her. Instead, she saw a fierce determination.

Amber turned back to the circle and

concentrated. She filled her mind with good things – her family and friends, the desert. She focused so hard that she didn't realize what was beginning to happen.

"Good," Stefan encouraged.

A gasp came up from the crowd as all eyes turned towards the roof.

"You're doing it!" said Harriet.

A few people screamed, fearing that the roof would roll over and take the lower seats down with it.

"Keep going!" urged Kayla.

"Amber, don't stop," added Jinx.

The roof was lifting.

The black knot inside Amber began to expand, getting larger and larger, as if fighting back the good thoughts she was thinking.

The roof began to shake and tremble, threatening to collapse again.

"I believe in you," Amber heard Christopher say. "In your strength."

The roof rose again. It looked like the wreck of a crashed spaceship attempting to blast off from an alien world.

The dark knot began to press against the inside of Amber's skin. She felt like a bubble about to burst.

"Go, Amber," called Elena.

"We love you!" Harriet murmured.

The roof shuddered above the crowd, casting everyone in shadow. Then it flipped into a clear area of the arena, landing in a pile of broken wood, mangled pipe, and crumpled steel beams.

The knot inside Amber exploded, hurling her to the ground.

Ambulance sirens wailed as police and emergency crews rushed to help the spectators as they were freed from the rubble. It was like a war zone, with the injured being rushed off on stretchers and loaded on to helicopters.

Through a delirious haze, Amber tried to focus on her parents and friends. "Is...is...?" she was barely able to utter.

"Everyone will be fine," Harriet murmured, cradling Amber in her arms.

"We're proud of you," Stefan said, tears forming in his eyes.

"Girlfriend, that was awesome!" shouted Kayla.

Amber heard none of them. Looking up at the cloudless western sky, her eyes rolled back into her head and she collapsed.

It took a full month, but the uproar finally began to die down. After an investigation, officials declared that a fluke weather phenomenon had caused the roof to come loose, flip over, and collapse. They said it was not unlike a wind shear which without warning can knock an airliner out of the sky.

Amateur photographers (who had taken their camcorders to the rodeo to capture sons and daughters in competition) even had it on video – the roof raising like a massive canopy filling with air, then somersaulting and disintegrating. The videos were seen on all of the local TV stations, and even made the nightly news on most of the major networks.

In the wake of the catastrophe, the school called in psychologists and social workers trained in trauma management, to meet with students and their families. No one had been killed, but many people were injured. The rodeo itself was rescheduled, allowing Troy and Brad and the others to fully recover from their injuries.

Law suits were filed left and right, against the showground, the school district, the county maintenance office – against just about everyone but the rodeo clowns. Legal experts

185

predicted the suits would take months, if not years, to settle.

Amber and her parents avoided the hubbub. They stayed close to home, happy to be by themselves. Relieved that the whole horrible episode was over. For the first time in months, they played chamber music written for three instruments, with Amber at the piano.

"So, Amber," Harriet said one Saturday morning at breakfast, "don't you miss your friends?"

"Yes, Amber, isn't it time you girls all got together?" added Stefan.

"To tell the truth," Amber said with a little grin, "I've kind of enjoyed the break. I think the five of us were spending too much time together."

Ever since the disaster, the word LASSO had never been uttered again by any of its five members. To emphasize to the other students at LA West that they were no longer a functioning group, the girls had deliberately avoided each other's company. The only friend that Amber ever saw was Jinx, and that was because they were riding partners at the ranch.

"Well, a little distance is probably a good thing," Harriet agreed. "Stefan and I have certainly enjoyed spending time with you. Especially since you've started work on your new science project."

"Photosynthesis may sound a little boring," Amber admitted. "but I really don't think I could even face the word telekinesis right now. It's still too upsetting."

"Photosynthesis is interesting and safe," observed Harriet, who was pouring herself some more coffee. "I like that."

"Dad, what time is it?" asked Amber.

Stefan glanced at his watch. "I can't tell you," he said. "It's stopped." He shook his wrist. "Darn this old wind-up thing! Mornings like this I wish I could wear a quartz watch!"

"It's almost ten," Harriet reported, looking at the oven clock. "Are you going to see Chris at the ranch?"

"I don't know," Amber said, dabbing at her lips with her napkin. "Jinx is picking me up. Maybe we'll run into him on our ride."

"I really wish you two could patch things up," said Stefan, still fiddling with his watch.

Amber shrugged. "I think he's being cautious. Just like everyone else. Ever since that rumour spread that I was responsible for what happened at the rodeo, there are kids at school who won't even come near me."

"Rumours fade," Harriet said, sitting back at the table. "The important thing is that you're feeling better."

"That weird dark knot inside me is gone," replied Amber with a sigh of relief.

Harriet and Stefan gave each other a quick glance. Amber raised a cautionary finger.

"I know that look," she said. "You two have doubts that it's gone for ever. But I promise – it's gone! I feel like a new person. I don't think I could put the slightest dent in a spoon. And I certainly couldn't lift anything."

"Forgive us, but we're scientists," Harriet responded. "I guess we're sceptical by nature."

"Well, this is one time when you don't have to be," Amber assured her parents.

A horn beeped outside.

"That must be Jinx." Amber leapt to her feet and carried her breakfast dishes to the kitchen counter. "We may grab a bite and catch a movie after the ride," she told her parents as she moved towards the door.

"Oh, Amber, you can't," Harriet called. "You need to come home right after riding."

Hearing this, Amber stopped short of the front door. "Why?" she shot back.

"Because I've made a big crockpot stew," Harriet replied. "Plus we're having the Briscoes over for lunch!"

"But I hate the Briscoes," Amber shouted. "And – no offence, Mom – but I *loathe* crockpot stew!"

"Amber, I'm sorry, but they're expecting to see you," Stefan insisted from the kitchen. "Tell Jinx you'll see her later tonight. Or tomorrow."

"Fine." Amber slammed her cowboy hat down on her head. "I hate stew, I hate the Briscoes," she grumbled as she threw open the front door. "Jinx and I were hoping to actually have some fun—but I'll be a good daughter and come home."

She paused in the doorway, waiting for them to say something. When they didn't, Amber shut the door behind her and raced to join Jinx.

Her parents hadn't responded because they were in shock.

Back in the kitchen, the crockpot loaded with stew had suddenly hurled itself against the wall. Harriet and Stefan stared in horror as great globs of stew trickled down the wall on to the tiled floor.

Globs tinted an angry, magnetic red.

ZODIAC

*ARIES*TAURUS*GEMINI*CANCER*LEO*VIRGO*LIBRA*
*SCORPIO*SAGITTARIUS*CAPRICORN*AQUARIUS*PISCES*

Twelve signs of the Zodiac. Twelve novels, each one embracing the characteristics of a zodiac sign. Pushed to the extreme, these characteristics lead down twisting paths into tales of mystery, horror, romance and fantasy.

Whatever your sun sign, you will want to read Zodiac, the series written in the stars.

SERIES CREATED BY JAHNNA N. MALCOLM

ZODIACS COMPLIMENTARY TO AQUARIUS...

PISCES:
A DREAMER, KNOWS SECRETS
SIXTH SENSE

*P*hoebe is a loner. She can sense when
something's wrong, but people distrust her
and are afraid of her premonitions. When
Mark Chenier disappears, images grow in
Phoebe's mind – she knows where Mark is,
but no one, except her Cajun grandmother,
believes her. Can she prove that she is right
and that her 'dreams' really tell the truth?

SAGITTARIUS:
DARING, HIGH-SPIRITED
STRANGE DESTINY

*S*kye is a star athlete. She's playing football
when she knocks her head and is concussed…
and wakes one hundred years ago, in the
middle of a mystery. Skye must return to the
present to find the key to the mystery - but she
doesn't want to leave someone she has met in
the past. Will she ever see him again?

CANCER:
EMOTIONAL, CARING
DARK SHADOWS

*C*hloe works tirelessly in her garden to create something beautiful, but nothing seems to flourish. Is it because a murderer used to live in the house before Chloe and her brother moved in? Then, a secret helper transforms the garden overnight – a secret helper who doesn't want Chloe to know his identity. Can the murder be linked to him and can caring Chloe put the pieces of the chain together?

LIBRA:
FAIR-MINDED, ROMANTIC
FROZEN IN TIME

*L*ily lives for her painting. With her boyfriend, she creates a mural that grows ever more beautiful as her own life becomes harsher. Then her boyfriend is killed by a gang. Has Lily lost him forever? If only she could be with him still in the beautiful world of the painting...